Critical acclaim for
THE LONG NIGHT OF FRANCI

"COMPELLING AND ULTIMATELY MOVING . . . full of humor and humanity, the only weapons that can kill the spirit of fascism."   —*Publishers Weekly*

"Deftly charted . . . a stark portrait of psychological terror."   —*Booklist*

"FASCINATING . . . a taut, timely political novel."
—*United Press International*

"Powerful and important . . . shines with simple freshness."   —*Baltimore Sun*

"Oblique political fiction, this—all the more effective for its top-layer of humor, which by contrast only increases the visceral brutality and deadliness of its underlying subject."   —*Kirkus Reviews*

"Reflects the same fears and concerns that most of us share . . . the very last page of the book is simply overwhelming."   —*Houston Chronicle*

HUMBERTO COSTANTINI was born in Buenos Aires in 1924. He is the highly acclaimed author of *The Gods, the Little Guys and the Police*, as well as several collections of short stories, books of poetry, and plays. He returned recently to Argentina after years of exile in Mexico City.

The Long Night of Francisco Sanctis

Humberto Costantini

Translated from the Spanish
by Norman Thomas di Giovanni

A PLUME BOOK

NEW AMERICAN LIBRARY

NEW YORK AND SCARBOROUGH, ONTARIO

This book was originally published in Argentina under the title *La larga noche de Francisco Sanctis*. Editorial Bruguera Argentina Safic © 1984.

Published by agreement with Harper & Row, Publishers, Inc.

Original hardcover edition designed by Sidney Feinberg

 PLUME TRADEMARK REG. U.S. PAT. OFF. AND FOREIGN COUNTRIES
REG. TRADEMARK—MARCA REGISTRADA
HECHO EN HARRISONBURG, VA., U.S.A.

SIGNET, SIGNET CLASSIC, MENTOR, ONYX, PLUME, MERIDIAN and NAL BOOKS
are published *in the United States* by New American Library,
1633 Broadway, New York, New York 10019, *in Canada* by
The New American Library of Canada Limited, 81 Mack Avenue,
Scarborough, Ontario M1L 1M8

Library of Congress Cataloging-in-Publication Data

Costantini, Humberto.
    The long night of Francisco Sanctis.

    Translation of: La larga noche de Francisco Sanctis.
    I. Title.
[PQ7798.13.O75L3713 1986]   863   86-18276
ISBN 0-452-25889-8 (pbk.)

First Plume Printing, October, 1986

1 2 3 4 5 6 7 8 9

PRINTED IN THE UNITED STATES OF AMERICA

CONTENTS

CHAPTER I

In which, so as to keep the reader from raising his hopes too high with regard to the entertainment value of this little book, it is here stated without further ado that its subject matter is of a more or less psychological nature—or, in other words, that the prospect ahead is fairly humdrum. Thus forewarned, the reader can now be told something about a certain telephone call that came from out of the blue

This is, when all is said and done, an account of an inner conflict—or, we could say, of a moral dilemma. The one suffered by Francisco Sanctis, an office worker, which began that early evening of Friday the eleventh of November 1977, and whose resolution (final, as it happens) was to cost him no fewer than ten valiant hours of wrestling with himself.

To claim that this inner struggle, this dilemma, arose out of a sudden eruption of his past into his present would amount to searching for a metaphysical dimension in a story that may not have one. Better, really, to say that it all began with a phone call from a certain girl—overweight, myopic, garrulous, and on the face of

new subject

1

it, a bit nutty as well—whom the man at first had great difficulty remembering and of whom he had had no news for something like the past seventeen years.

The roly-poly girl—Elena was her name—had in some way or other found out the telephone number of Luchini & Monsreal, the small grocery wholesalers where Sanctis worked, and on that Friday, at five o'clock, she rang him there.

A detail which may be amusing or plain silly but that should nevertheless be pointed out: The girl had asked for Mr. Francisco Sanctis, first of the switchboard, then of González, who sat at the next desk, yet when González absently handed him the receiver, Sanctis heard a woman's voice, suggestive in a very forced way, asking whether the person on the line (that's exactly what she said, as if she were speaking from Stockholm) was Leonardo Medina. Thinking it a mistake, Sanctis replied, "Sorry, miss, wrong number," and he started to hang up, when the voice let out a hint of a giggle and said, "Then you don't remember me anymore?" In response to Sanctis's slightly irritated no, and feeling he was about to put down the receiver, she blurted out the name of an obscure literary magazine that had barely survived two issues, then went on about a gathering in the house of a Socialist congressman and a public demonstration on Callao Street that got out of hand and during the course of which she and Sanctis had taken turns carrying a placard. Then the rehearsals of a play that was never put on, and finally her name—Elena. Elena Vaccaro, from the School of Liberal Arts, who traveled in every day all the way from Ciudadela, who belonged to a street theater group out in La Matanza. Elena Vaccaro— a name, so she claimed, closely linked to Leonardo Medina's in the first issue of that undergraduate publication.

At this point things began growing clearer. And suddenly from some recess of Francisco Sanctis's mind sprang the girl's name as well as Leonardo Medina's, linked—or at any rate placed side by side—with Elena Vaccaro's in that first issue of the all-but-forgotten magazine.

For he recalled that "Leonardo Medina" was the pen name (a bit stagy, a bit lowbrow, he now admitted) with which the young Francisco Sanctis had signed the only two things he had ever published: an article of sorts— hotheaded, dripping with rhetoric, very short—about the universal suppression of ideas, and clearly inspired by the ornate prose of José Ingenieros; and a free-verse poem in which love for a woman got mixed up just a touch arbitrarily with a rail strike and a dying afternoon in Palermo. As for Elena—yes, of course, Elena Vaccaro was that fat girl with boundless energy who wore glasses, a liberal arts major, the magazine's business manager, an appalling actress, a political activist belonging (as far as one knew) to some left-wing splinter group. Sanctis had a dim memory of her in which a certain mercurial quality at times got mixed up with obstinacy and even absurdity. Then a sharper picture of her began to emerge: her thick-lensed glasses, the way she walked with the stride and grace of a camel, her shoes, which had all the appearance of either having been issued by a reform school or designed by an orthopedic surgeon, and her voice, unpleasant, high-pitched, nasal, and quite distinct—Sanctis couldn't help noting—from the deep, well-modulated, and slightly seductive one speaking now out of the telephone about magazines, gatherings, and street demonstrations.

And once plunged into remembering, he remembered, too, that for a short spell the fleshy Elena—you didn't have to be overly brainy to see it—was more or less in love with Sanctis, or rather with Leonardo Medina, that master of amatory-inflammatory verses. But Sanctis, who had warded off as best he could the fat girl's rather naive and all too obvious advances, and who at the same time was himself head over heels in love with a certain local girl—she was wonderful, she was inaccessible, she was Armenian—had kept up friendly relations with Elena that, although a mite protective or paternal, were strictly within the realm of the would-be political activities of the day. These amounted to the time-consuming editing of the magazine; marches in support of secular schools; student gatherings; and the rendezvous in their haunt at the corner of Córdoba and Pasteur, which now flocked unerringly to his memory mingled with the nostalgic taste of ham-and-cheese specials cut from crusty French loaves.

And so when Sanctis at last found out who this was phoning him at the offices of Luchini & Monsreal, completely out of the blue, he couldn't help but respond to the evocative effect of the tubby Elena's words with po-

lite and even heartfelt interjections of surprise. Still—
and he didn't know exactly why—a slight uneasiness
nagged at him from some quarter. It wasn't really serious. Something, say, on the order of finding himself, at
a parents night at his children's school, all at once face
to face with some barfly with whom he once got drunk.
Or turn it around. As if at a get-together of his office or
drinking cronies, who should suddenly appear but Father
Ramírez, his prefect when Sanctis was a seminarian,
wanting to talk to him about the sin of lust and the way
to fight it. In other words, something that didn't quite
mesh, that somehow upset the natural order of things.
Maybe, he thought, it was no more than the creepy sensation of hearing himself called Leonardo Medina when
Francisco Sanctis now headed up the accounting department at Luchini & Monsreal, was married, with three
kids, and at long last on the right track financially, had
never written another poem and still less been involved
in politics since that time long out of mind which old
roly-poly here was bent (why?) on reviving. All that
went back, he reckoned, to 1959 or 1960. Between him
and that confused, restless boy—the former seminarian,
the unsuccessful medical student involved in university
literary magazines, the author of earth-shaking essays on
the suppression of intellectual freedom, the bearer of
placards in support of secular education—lay more than
seventeen years.

Francisco Sanctis of course told Elena sure, he remembered her very well, and he lied that he'd often wondered
how she was getting on and that he even remembered

almost line for line her outstanding, original contribution to that first number of their magazine (an interview with Manauta on Argentine writing and on politically committed writers—that sort of thing).

He heard her thanking him for his praises, then clearing her throat as if she, too, wasn't quite comfortable with certain memories, and then hesitating for several seconds before saying, in a voice that seemed to Sanctis uncertain, "Well, as a matter of fact, now that you bring up the magazine, that's just what I wanted to speak to you about."

"Really? But what about?" Sanctis asked, frankly amused, preparing to listen to the most monumental piece of tripe.

Another throat-clearing, another short span of silence, another "Well, as a matter of fact" (which served simultaneously to introduce the next remark and, of course, to give her time to think of what to say), and then, "As a matter of fact, I really have to talk to you in person. By phone it's . . . it's a bit complicated, you see?"

Oh, no, my dear, thought Sanctis. If you're going to come on like this we won't get anywhere. Without disguising his irritation, he told her he didn't see what was so complicated about talking the thing over by telephone. Two or three times he interrupted Elena's dithering explanations. In fact, he was on the point of telling her to stop beating around the bush and come straight out with what was on her mind. In the end she did.

"It's about that poem you published—you remember it?" Elena said, but to Sanctis she seemed tentative, unconvincing, as if she were making the whole thing up as she spoke. "It . . . it seems they want to print it in a magazine."

"Oh? What magazine?"

"A magazine—a Venezuelan magazine. So of course they need your permission. Have you any objection?"

"No, why should I? But what magazine is it?" Sanctis asked pointedly, forcing her to go on with her tale.

"An important one . . . How can I put it? It's strictly slick, not like the one we used to publish. Its name slips my mind right now. But it's not political, I assure you."

It was a piece of humbug typical of Elena Vaccaro. Sanctis was beginning to lose what remained of his patience. If what this nut wanted was to see him, shit, couldn't she have come up with something better? Even a plain "I want to see you" would have done the trick. But to spew out all this romantic twaddle was to treat him like a prize idiot. Who else would have dreamed up the notion that some mysterious magazine—one of the leading slicks—urgently required the permission of the unknown Francisco Sanctis in order to publish a nonentity of a poem written seventeen years earlier? No one but Elena Vaccaro.

Still, for a split second, a wave of gullibility or folly had him thinking that the story might just be true. Why not? Such things happen—they do in the movies. He wondered what sort of magazine it might be. Maybe Elena herself had sent a copy of their publication to Venezuela, and people there thought Sanctis was somebody famous, and somehow . . .

7

But this possibility, so absurd and so remote, instead of cheering him, troubled and even depressed him. It was as if Father Taglioretti, his algebra teacher at the seminary, had stopped by the office to tell him that now, at the age of forty-one, he had passed his final exam. Or as if Zulema (the wonderful, inaccessible local girl, today overblown, frowsy, and the mother of a swarm of offspring) were to appear at his door to grant him her retroactive consent.

A lapse, of course, a moment of excusable stupidity, and he at once regained his senses. He wanted to put an end to this thing as soon as possible. To make matters worse, that idiot González, sitting there just six feet away, hadn't missed a single word of the conversation. He pretended to be working, naturally; his nose was buried in his books and now and then he jotted figures on a slip of paper. Yes, but he was taking great pains not to use the calculator, not wanting its clatter to interfere with the soap opera, and once or twice Sanctis saw González's mustache curl into a smirk.

For the time being, better agree to anything, wind up the conversation without further ado, and put down the phone.

"All right, then, Elena. I give you my authorization. Do as you like with the thing." (He said "thing" instead of "poem" only because of González's mustache.) Okay, now the goodbye. "And please excuse me, but I'm up to my ears in work." He thought that a bit curt, so added, "Give me your number. What I'll do is phone you later on from home, when I'm not so frantic. How's that?"

Well-chosen, persuasive words that would get him out from under with relative grace. But no. Again the hesitations and throat-clearings, and suddenly, *wham!* one below the belt to test all his skill and patience. For here was Elena completely taken aback that he didn't know that permission of this kind had to be in writing and duly signed by the author himself.

"As I said, it's a serious magazine, so, you see . . ."

Sanctis shot González a look out of the corner of his eye and said hurriedly, his voice low, "Okay, Monday, then. All right? Phone me in the afternoon and we can meet somewhere around here, downtown, right after work. And I'm sorry, but I've got to hang up now."

"It can't be Monday," Elena cut in sharply, and for the first time her voice revealed something akin to haste or anxiety. "It has to be today, don't you understand?"

Understand what? thought Sanctis, but he took care not to ask the question aloud, so as not to extend the conversation. He said simply, "It so happens that I've got a lot on today, kiddo, and there's no way I can manage it."

"Listen," said Elena, on the attack, and at once her voice took on all the assurance of an executive. "I'm not going to rob you of more than a half hour of your time. Where do you have to be?"

"In Belgrano. Near my place. At nine sharp." Sanctis found himself answering her questions like a schoolboy. He felt pretty foolish. Changing his tone, he added, "You see how things stand, so really, then . . . well, I don't see how we can manage it. Monday's much better, don't you

9

agree? Besides, from what you say, it can't be all that urgent, so—"

"That's okay," Elena cut in again. "Eight o'clock, then, at the corner of Cabildo and Juramento. All right?"

"All right," Sanctis said, and, resigned and annoyed with himself, he hung up.

González began punching away at the calculating machine.

CHAPTER II

About how a printed tie from the fifties and the seductive odor of Vitalis hair tonic momentarily replace the conflicting taste of ham-and-cheese specials

At twenty minutes to eight, Sanctis—who, to kill time, got off his bus half a dozen blocks before the appointed meeting place—was walking very slowly along Cabildo, crossing Pampa in the direction of Juramento.

Now, after deep, straphanging reflection, he was completely convinced that the whole business of the poem and the Venezuelan magazine was sheer invention on the part of Miss Roly-Poly, that what this dizzy Elena Vaccaro had in mind must be something quite different and obviously a lot more complicated than the simple-minded nonsense she was trying to peddle.

So he wanted to feel relaxed, comfortable, sure of himself. Any other way and the pushy fat girl would catch him off guard. But who could relax loaded down like a pack horse? For in addition to his briefcase and the record of Corelli concerti grossi played by Isaac Stern, which he had bought that lunchtime at Ricordi's, Sanctis was also carrying, goddamn it, a heavy package—in it, eight different cans of this and that which his wife at the last minute had asked him to bring home. After writing up a slip for them, he'd got them himself out of Luchini & Monsreal's storeroom. It seemed absurd, but the fact of not having a hand to scratch one's nose or to tug at one's crotch gave him—like it or not—an uneasy feeling, part insecurity, part awkwardness. More so because he had no idea how long the little talk with Elena was going to take. No more than a half hour, she'd said, but how was one to know such things in advance?

As a matter of fact, his unpostponable nine o'clock engagement was partly a lie. It had simply been the first excuse he could dream up for giving her the slip that night. It was undeniable that he might be seeing the Crespis later on, but the arrangement, which wasn't at all firm, had come up as a possibility only that morning, when he bumped into Fernando in the corridor of their apartment house. Knowing that Fernando Crespi, who lived on the floor below, was, like him, fond of music, Sanctis said (casually, a bit offhand) as the two were walking to the street door that one of these nights Fernando and his wife should drop in, listen to some records, have coffee, and, at the same time, take a look at the new stereo with earphones and four professional-type JBM speakers that Sanctis had just bought for his living room.

Crespi, perhaps because he felt under some sort of obligation, had said yes, he was delighted, and, a bit offhand himself, had answered that maybe they'd make it that same night, or possibly Saturday night, provided he didn't get back too late from a certain meeting he was attending and his wife recovered from her bout of flu. That was it. In other words, nothing was fixed for nine o'clock sharp, nor was it sure the Crespis would turn up at all. Therefore, the meeting with little Elena Vaccaro could be drawn out a bit if need be.

Sanctis had almost said to himself, "If there's anything in it," but out of the treacherous smog of memory there she was, that ball-breaking, four-eyed roly-poly with the vaguely blond hair, the camel-like slope, and the ever-present bag dangling from her shoulder. On the spot he made up his mind that their meeting had no reason to be drawn out even a second more than necessary—that is, coffee or a drink at the Mignon, the problem of keeping little tubby to the point, a straight answer to her request or proposal or whatever the hell it was, and on to something else. Steering clear, of course, of birdbrained involvement in other people's muddles— least of all those of a loony like Elenita Vaccaro, whose widespread fame as a tale-spinner and mythomaniac stretched way back to their magazine days.

Once more he switched the infernal package from one hand to the other. Its fraying cord had cut into his flesh, leaving a nice purple indentation. He also felt his fingers going stiff and numb. Try as he might, owing to the bulk and the number of the things he was carrying, he was unable to flex his hand, and he ended up in a bizarre, twisted, and altogether ridiculous stance. A stance and consequent state of mind that couldn't have been in greater contrast to those of the Francisco Sanctis of his imagination, so swift and sure, who in no time at all, right there among the tables of the Mignon, would set things straight with Miss Roly-Poly. Yet the whole thing bothered him. Not because he was out to make an impression on Elena Vaccaro—not at all. It was obvious that this meeting had nothing to do with a pickup or anything of the kind. But—he didn't know why exactly—a wisp of a voice deep inside told him that he had to appear before Elena Vaccaro armed to the teeth. This precaution was not unjustified. Who knew what improbable story she'd come out with and, as a result, what exhaustive means he would have to employ not to be caught in the tangled web of her craziness.

Because obviously no one was going to swallow this story about the poem and the important Venezuelan magazine—so important she couldn't remember its name. Nothing but a pretext, and a bad one at that, for getting this meeting out of him—dreamed up, he'd swear, in the course of their ridiculous telephone conversation. He could almost pinpoint it. It was when, just to say something, he'd mentioned the interview with Manauta. *Wham!* At that very point she seized on his words and then, by a simple association of ideas, the thing about the magazine and the poem had come to her. So unless he didn't mind passing himself off as an idiot, this business of the Venezuelan magazine had to be put out of mind from the very start.

Then what? What reason was there for a woman like her, someone he barely knew, in fact, to find out his phone number at work and call him, which in itself was

14

a bit fishy, and then to order him—yes, order him—to meet her that same day, all because of some extremely urgent and unpostponable foul-up?

The old flame rekindled? Come on, he told himself, glancing down on the makings of a potbelly, are we to believe we're the Rudolph Valentino of Monroe Street now? That infatuation Elena had for him all those years ago couldn't have shit to do with this situation. Besides—it was pointless not keeping simple things simple—her crush, hots, fancy, or whatever it was involved not him but the eminent poet Leonardo Medina, that nonexistent Romeo on whom the inexperienced teenage tubby had bestowed who knew what romantic attributes.

He continued walking along Cabildo, and in spite of having quit smoking upon medical advice some four months earlier, he stopped at a kiosk and bought cigarettes and matches. But he didn't light one up. He just wanted, needed, to have the pack of king-size filter-tipped Imparciales nicely tucked away in an inside pocket of his jacket. To have them—only to have them. He imagined that the presence of the familiar little package, there on his left side just above the belt, added in some way to his self-assurance and poise. He imagined that at the right moment the little package might prove useful.

And apparently this was already happening. For in passing a shopwindow he caught himself sucking in his belly and trying—to no avail, since the annoying parcels prevented it—to tighten the knot of his tie.

The situation had its amusing side. Which was that

now—after a long bus ride from Luchini & Monsreal, after González's insufferable, whiskery sneer—the imminent meeting with a woman, however overweight, ungainly, and myopic she might be, once again had about it a quality of mystery, of magic, of the unpredictable. Something in common with those youthful encounters of his, brimming with anticipation, that he still remembered as an intermingling of sensations, clear in detail yet often not entirely explicable. In this particular case, it was not the taste of ham-and-cheese specials, as in the days of their magazine and militancy, but something farther removed in time and a lot subtler—the softly muted red of a certain necktie (of Bulgarian design, it was claimed) and the distinct odor of Vitalis hair tonic as it gradually permeated the house from a tiny mirror beside the backyard patio washbasin. Something, in short, which, like the suave signature tune of a soap opera, prophetically announced the stairway to the stars that, more and more, he was prepared to take—why not?—if the opportunity presented itself. This, naturally, in the event that Elena's looks had improved—her figure, that is—as, obviously, her voice had. Because Elena's voice, now that he remembered it, really had improved. It was no longer that parakeet's screech one had found so immediately irritating. Now it was a true woman's voice—deep, deliberate, suggestive. Boy, had Elenita's voice improved in seventeen years!

And so it was, alas, that Francisco Sanctis forgot all his wise precautions against Elena Vaccaro, and on the dot of eight, briefcase and phonograph record in one hand, parcel of canned goods in the other, his defenses dangerously down, he planted himself like a good little boy at the busy street corner of Cabildo and Juramento.

No printed tie of the fifties adorned his neck, true enough, but it must be admitted that amid the foul smell of exhaust coming off the street and the smell of reheated coffee drifting through the Mignon's doors, it was possible to detect the scent—slight, unmistakable, and romantic—of Vitalis hair tonic.

CHAPTER III

In which, as a certain parcel of canned goods changes hands a dozen times and in view of the fact that punctuality seems not to be Elena Vaccaro's chief virtue, an attempt is made to while away these tedious minutes by telling a little more about Francisco Sanctis

Francisco Nicodemus Sanctis ("son of Carmine Sanctis and Assunta Gambardella, born in Buenos Aires on the fourth of October 1936," so his birth certificate recorded) at the age of twelve was a quiet, introverted child. Since he spent hours lying about reading, and as, unlike the majority of boys his age, he never made a fuss when his parents asked him to attend church, they (particularly doña Assunta, a bossy, shrewd, devout, ignorant Neapolitan) decided quite naturally that their son had a religious vocation.

So, having completed his primary education with no major hitches, upon the recommendation of a certain Father Cioppi, a fellow townsman of doña Assunta's, her confessor, and the family's spiritual adviser, Francisco Nicodemus Sanctis found himself out at the far end of the city as a boarder at the Villa Devoto Seminary.

Nor had young Sanctis any major hitches at the demanding seminary—not in his first three years, at least. He was fairly studious, he faithfully carried out his duties, he extended his retreats longer than was prescribed, he wrote long letters home (supervised, of course, by his prefect), in which he spoke of God, of spiritual peace, of Divine Providence, and of the deep happiness he derived from all his tasks. The letters, though written in a dull, protocolic style, were looked upon by doña Assunta as the epitome of scholarship, of goodness, and of wisdom, and they were proudly shown to Father Cioppi and to every neighbor within range of the family's fruit and vegetable shop on Manuela Pedraza Street out in Villa Urquiza.

But midway through his fourth year it came to pass that Sanctis suffered what first his spiritual adviser and later the heads of the seminary called a crisis of faith. He failed four subjects, he napped during retreats, and in his letters home, now brief and few and far between, he mostly spoke of his health, which at the time was dubious. He must have fallen into other kinds of transgression as well (which, in fact, were never clearly spelled out), because one day don Carmine Sanctis received a letter from the rector, informing him that the young Francisco Nicodemus Sanctis, "of his own free will," had resigned from the seminary.

The fact, not all that earth-shaking in itself, launched the family into a kind of Greek tragedy. Added to their howls of purest south Italian grief were the bewilderment of not knowing exactly what had taken place, the frustration of seeing ancestral aspirations go down the drain, and a smoldering resentment toward the adolescent Francisco, who, in some no doubt disgraceful way, had stained the family honor.

Actually, old don Carmine was only awaiting the green light of doña Assunta's approval so that he could wade in as God and the implacable spirit of his forebears ordained. But after having soaked through several dozen handkerchiefs, doña Assunta, forsaking her "miserable lot" and fittingly tearing her hair, opted for grim silence. An outraged silence, a martyr's silence, a thousand times more damaging—as life was later to prove—than the after all unimportant thrashing that don Carmine the fruit vendor had been prepared to administer.

Because from then on—and this has to be underlined—Francisco Sanctis lived by and large in the persecutory shadow of his mother's silent, sinister accusation. As if the guilt he took upon himself for failing in his career as a priest weren't enough, doña Assunta's mute reproach (it came out strategically in pained sighs, or in words mumbled supposedly to herself in some kind of incomprehensible Neapolitan, or in references of seeming little importance yet whose barbs hit him like deadly wing shots) drove him to feel he was the most despicable creature on earth—part idiot, part lecherous monster, part bloodthirsty parricide. These events took place when he was sixteen, the year that poor Francisco Nicodemus needed extra help in coping with the terrible shock that his entering high school turned out to be and from which, to tell the truth, he never quite recovered.

Contrary to the expectation of some of his teachers, who knew about his record as a seminarian, and in spite of having entered second year at Mariano Moreno High from his fourth year at the seminary, Francisco Nicodemus Sanctis was a mediocre and at times a hopeless student.

Perhaps the difficult process of adapting to this new world of after-school poolrooms, smutty stories, football, fistfights, and first sexual experiences received his best energies. The fact was that what with repeating exams and getting second chances and using crib sheets, he just managed to squeak through and earn a diploma.

Nineteen at the time, on the thin side, clothes-conscious, an occasional frequenter of cheap dance halls, a habitué of the downtown Café La Paz, a holder of no political views, he had more or less decided he should pursue a university career—law maybe, or medicine, or economics—get a degree, and settle down.

It was at this juncture that he began adopting the manner, soft-spoken and slightly world-weary, half tough, half dandy, of the old-time hoodlums of outer Buenos Aires, and with it a matching vocabulary steeped in slang. A vocabulary and manner (although familiar enough to him during his childhood in Villa Urquiza, completely buried during his years at the seminary) that in observance of mysterious laws suddenly came alive again after he finished high school and never, in spite of fundamental changes in his life after that, completely left him.

Don Carmine's small fruit and vegetable shop had done well in those last few years (pushed by doña Assunta, he'd bought the shop next to his, had hired two employees, and was driving the latest model Ford pickup), so that Francisco felt duty bound to go to university.

Still, it must be said (because this has to do with his future life as well as with a certain struggle he will have to come to grips with at the age of forty-one, which, as we know, is what this story is about) that the reputation he enjoyed among his friends as a happy-go-lucky rake (the victorious culmination, so to speak, of his long, hard process of adapting) was justified only in part. Although it was true that enjoying a bit of pocket money, dressing well, and having no financial obligations to his family allowed him certain not always innocent amusements, the fact was that in some ways Francisco Sanctis had about him a good deal of the onetime theology student or, rather, of the naive, spiritual boy of those first years at the seminary. He was conscience-stricken about having no vocation, he found it hard putting up with the hypocritical business world around him, and vague ideas about what was socially moral and immoral were beginning to gnaw at him.

Perhaps it was owing to this—to a certain deep need which neither his high-school life, nor the gatherings at the café, nor the sprees, nor the sporadic pickups, had satisfied—that after a lot of vacillation and a year and a half lost shuttling in and out of one departmental office after another, he enrolled as a medical student. That was back around 1957, and almost straightaway he approached one of those student groups which, each in its own fashion, were struggling for the democratization of the country and for changes in the social structure, while simultaneously trying to expose the infiltration of fascism into the universities. Fighting, in short, for ideas to which Francisco Sanctis felt immediately and spontaneously drawn—maybe only because to him they stood for the opposite of all he'd lived in the preceding years, which, he now realized, was nothing but a long, patient, and at times painful effort on his part to join a world that somewhere deep inside he looked down on.

It must be admitted that this was a good period for young Francisco Sanctis. A period of feverish activity; of exhausting meetings; of agitated gatherings in which, little by little, he learned to make himself heard by his comrades; of demonstrations; of slogan painting; of the hasty creation of banners and placards; of student elections; of friendships born in the heat of these enthusiasms; of a newborn prestige he'd never dreamed of having—that of a clear-thinking polemicist. It was also the period of their little magazine (*Fist on High*, it was called), founded by "a group of young people united in one and the same poetical, revolutionary zeal," as their first editorial proclaimed. The magazine's five hundred copies were distributed by hand at the entrances of various university buildings, and in its badly laid out pages, as we already know, Leonardo Medina published his complete literary works.

And, of course, this was the time he met (briefly, as a matter of fact, and almost without any real personal contact) Elena Vaccaro. The same Elena Vaccaro who today, after seventeen years, not only showed she remembered his complete works but even had the dumb idea of calling him by his forgotten pen name.

This whole period lasted no more than a couple of years—a kind of spirited, necessary, heady parenthesis, no doubt, in the middle of a rather monotonous, colorless existence such as the one Francisco Sanctis led before and after.

Naturally, his university career couldn't help but suffer a bit as a result of all this. A failing grade in anatomy and a reactionary stinker of a section leader got him bogged down in his first year. Possibly he would have gone on in medicine for somewhat longer as a chronic student had his situation at home not taken a drastic turn.

CHAPTER IV

In which, as nothing has changed—that is to say, Elena Vaccaro has yet to make her appearance—we continue the story of Francisco Sanctis's life, trying, of course, to keep it short, since it's now twenty past eight and Elena Vaccaro may arrive at any moment

Don Carmine died early in 1959, and doña Assunta, who in spite of her long resentment by no means wanted to see her only son selling fruit and vegetables, took a loss on the shop and retired to a dignified and, from the pecuniary viewpoint, manageable widowhood. But little by little, inflation raised havoc with doña Assunta's savings. The pickup truck went first, and a house that don Carmine had bought outside the city in Santos Lugares, then an acre or two of land in Chilavert. Along the way, she made a few poor investments, so that all at once what she thought would carry her comfortably through the rest of her days turned out barely enough to scrape by on.

Without much regret, Francisco Sanctis quit medical school and got a job. But it wasn't easy. Those couple of years of university political action and his recently discovered humanitarian leanings, although haphazardly exercised, left their stamp on him. Not to mention his years at the seminary, which had left theirs as well. He despised the world of business, at the same time feeling he was unqualified for manual work. Offices bored him, and his fellow workers struck him as either idiots or mediocrities. It goes without saying that from a mile off his bosses smelled his unhealthy attitude, the fact that his mind was always on something else, and Francisco Sanctis never held down a job for long.

To make things worse, in 1965, a few months after doña Assunta died, when at last he thought he'd found a steady job, he got married. The job lasted exactly four months and twenty-one days.

He became, in succession, a clerk in an accountant's office, a jobber of bicycle parts, a distributor of pharmaceutical samples, a self-employed door-to-door peddler of perfumery, then the employee of a customs dispatcher, then a salesman again, and various things that never lasted long and that always, for some reason or other, left him with the bitter taste of failure and incompetence whenever he was fired.

In 1972, Francisco Sanctis—who had separated (stormily) from his first wife and whose second wife, María Angélica, had two children by a previous marriage—had with the latter his first and only child. His financial straits were as dire as ever.

It was owing to this, perhaps, to his constant worry about trying to make ends meet, that Francisco Sanctis finished up having nothing to do not only with former social and literary concerns but also with the political events that at the time were rising like a tide and shaking the country. Resistance to the military dictatorship, the massacre of guerrillas at Trelew, the certainty that young people different from those he had known— bolder and more generous—were making their voices heard by acts of sheer courage and, so it seemed, by a total dedication to their ideals (ideals only in part familiar to Sanctis): these things he was aware of. It would be foolish to say he wasn't. But news of these happenings reached him as if through a glass darkly. Via the newspapers or television, he learned about a murder committed by Triple A terrorists, about a strike, about an action of one of those groups termed subversive (he was never altogether clear about their complicated acronyms), and there were moments when he was moved or happy or indignant. But his happiness or indignation might as well have been produced by events that were taking place in Indochina or Biafra. In other words, for reasons only partly explicable (he was quite ready to admit it was a question of age), he felt he was standing on the sidelines. He felt he was a sort of spectator, let us say—a simple, part-time spectator of events—during the little free time he could count on after the monotonous routine of keeping his head above water in a world that seemed to reject him and into which he had trouble fitting as once, or so it appeared, he had managed to fit into the world of high school. That world struck him as violent and obscene then, though far less cruel and hypocritical than the world he lived in now.

And it occurred to him that in some intricate, round-about way, this detachment, this nonparticipation in what was going on, left him feeling disgruntled and to a certain extent ashamed. Without admitting it even to himself, he felt guilty. Guilty of what? It was hard to explain. Of insensitivity maybe, of not caring: guilt because some part of himself was slowly rusting up. A part which in the past (let's be honest, the days of his militancy and the magazine) had throbbed, or so it felt to him, with . . . with something that he couldn't exactly pinpoint but that stood for History, or the country, or people, or maybe just something more open, cleaner, more generous than his miserable everyday world.

Or maybe it was that their aims were more moral than political then, appealing more to Francisco Sanctis the individual than to his desires to change radically a society he considered unjust. What he felt as the gradual despiritualization of his life, caused by being perpetually engulfed in the problems of eking out a living, made him look on himself as a species of traitor to God knows what. Now in his forties and the father of three children, he was once again the absentminded, guilty boy—the one doña Assunta silently blamed—who, having lost his faith, felt obliged to leave the seminary in shame.

Still, one has to recognize that this dark sense of shame or guilt, which he kept to himself, never led him into neuroses, much less into making rash decisions. For the sake of family stability, his readiness to adjust and fit into the very world he once looked down on increased as the years passed. His bosses no longer considered him a queer fish, his fellow workers began to be fellow workers simply and not that moron Frías or that idiot Gutiérrez or that half-ass Piotti. At long last, life stopped being a doomed contest with a dreaded, lurking monster and changed into something he could bear, into a habit that was not so uncomfortable after all.

The cause, or even the consequence, of this healthy and necessary assimilation was his job with Luchini & Monsreal, where he'd been working—unbelievably—for three years now. It should be said in explanation that the firm's owners, the Genoese as much as the Catalan, regarded him from the beginning (he never really understood why) with particular esteem. They had brought his salary up to the level of their oldest employees, but more than anything else, from his first day at work they had made him feel comfortable and respected. That was something he'd never before felt in any of his long line of previous jobs.

His knowledge of bookkeeping, picked up working in an accountant's office, a painstaking dedication to whatever he undertook (he was fully aware that he was no longer a boy and that if he wanted to mend his ways he had to hang on to this job), and, particularly, the kindness he found all around him among the small staff of only a dozen or so on the office side, quickly transformed Francisco Sanctis into an employee of some importance. He was named, a bit pompously, Head of the Accounting Department (made up, as a matter of fact, of González and two other younger men), he was paid periodic bonuses, and it was hinted that in the coming year he might even be made a partner.

Naturally, his home life changed. With a steady income, Sanctis was at last able to pay off the mortgage on the Monroe Street apartment, send his children to a good school, encourage María Angélica to take up her piano studies again after an interruption of six years, and buy himself on credit what he'd longed for all his life—a really first-rate stereo, beside which, earphones on his head, he spent the best part of his weekends, listening to classical music.

This last thing, music, was a kind of all-purpose remedy for his problems. His worries about despiritualization, self-betrayal, and so forth—which had once caused him endless agonizing—began gradually and almost completely to disappear. For unquestionably, in spite of the long, full days he worked at Luchini & Monsreal, Francisco Sanctis had somehow come round again to his old humanitarian concerns. He loved music passionately, he was truly a connoisseur, and during those moments alone in his apartment when he melted in raptures over the performances of Ruggiero Ricci or Bernard Haitink, he felt himself transported to regions where he was intimately connected with the best of the human spirit, regions infinitely removed from his office routine, from his kids' problems at school, from María Angélica's cystitis, from the bathroom plumbing—from everything, in short, that insidiously attempted to drag him back into that petty world of everyday cares he had at long last surmounted.

The newspapers and television still spoke to him of a world of naked power, violence, and injustice. A world

30

in which the young, whom he readily admitted were heroic, were battling against the unlimited might of the armed forces. But for Francisco Sanctis the spectator, that was just it—it was a battle involving the young, the young of whom he could no longer feel a part but on whom he looked now and again with just a touch of sympathy, of nostalgia. And he attached no shame to this distance he felt from them—not anymore. He told himself that he, too, had done his bit and that it was only natural that another generation should want to keep those ideals alive now. So he had no reason to feel the slightest remorse for not participating in the present struggle. In his own way, he had regrouped his forces to concentrate on another kind of struggle, more individualistic, perhaps, and less heroic, but—careful, now—no less pitted against falsehood, utilitarianism, or oppression. Against spiritual annihilation, in a word.

In any case, supposing he wanted to, he hadn't the faintest idea how you even approached these young people. Things had changed so much since the days of the magazine and their marches in favor of secular education. Everything was so mysterious, so secret now. Who the hell knew how to get some form of support or at least some word through to them?

Once, at a small party in the house of friends, he had tried speaking about this to Lucho, the Fernándezes' eldest son, whom María Angélica suspected of being mixed up with one of those groups with the impossible acronyms. But the boy was quick to sidestep the conversation, and he left Sanctis standing there sadly, looking like a busybody or an utter fool. Besides, who knew if Lucho hadn't taken him for a spy or something.

So he never again attempted such a thing. It was clear that today's youth were going to ignore him, that they had no use for him. All right. He'd concentrate on his own struggle, then—music. Because for Francisco Sanctis music was more than a mere refuge or the search for his own salvation. It was in a sense his personal battle against a despicable commercial society that was trying to destroy him and that he believed he was giving the finger to with every phonograph record he played.

The fact was that after years of suffering the slings and arrows of a society with which he was obviously out of step, and without falling back on either confessor or psychoanalyst, Francisco Sanctis had now at the age of forty-one arrived at a well-deserved inner peace, a kind of wise and healthy equilibrium. It was unlikely that something or somebody could possibly upset the laws of this balance he had fought so hard to win.

CHAPTER V

In which, Francisco Sanctis's story concluded at last—at least until the eleventh of November 1977—something can be told about what's happening and, unfortunately, not happening inside a Renault 4L

Here, then, is Francisco Sanctis, Head of the Accounting Department of Luchini & Monsreal (Wholesalers), whom an all but forgotten overweight girl has addressed by a certain dusty pen name and prevailed on to agree to this meeting—this extremely urgent, unpostponable meeting—at the corner of Cabildo and Juramento.

But, as can be seen, urgency for Elena Vaccaro has a fairly broad meaning. It's now twenty-five minutes to nine, and Elena Vaccaro gives no sign of life.

Francisco Sanctis gets hot under the collar, and not just for being left in the lurch like this. These are no times, he thinks, to be standing here like an imbecile, planted on this street corner for thirty-five minutes, when there could be any number of cops in civilian clothes around, some probably watching him right now. And as if that weren't enough, here's this weird package hanging from one hand and about to split open and make

33

quite a lovely display of cans all over the thronging sidewalk. It would have made a lot more sense, of course, to meet inside the Mignon. But who'd have dreamed that after all the rush she was in and her coming on like some hotshot executive type, this nut was going to leave him stuck here like this, so humiliatingly let down. For another thing, he hadn't even had time to choose the spot. She'd been the one—that nut case Elena Vaccaro—who in her rather high-handed way had decided on where and when they would meet.

For a moment he considers ducking into the Mignon and waiting there. But glancing at the time, he decides simply to leave. Shit on this, he says to himself. Another of the four-eyed roly-poly's usual and well-known lunacies, more than likely, since she's obviously still the same histrionic, mythomaniac snake charmer and little fool of seventeen years ago. Hadn't she once come up with a story that two guys with faces like lugs (she was absolutely convinced they were CIA agents) were following her all over Buenos Aires? Why hadn't it occurred to him before starting out for this crazy meeting to take into account something as fundamental as those old obsessions of Elena Vaccaro's?

Out of sheer habit now he casts one last glance along the Cabildo sidewalk and begins to cross Juramento. Just then, behind him, he hears a series of short *ch-ch-ch* sounds like a little bird.

He turns. From the side window of a Renault 4L pulled up a couple of yards wide of the curb, a dark-haired woman with an angular face partly hidden behind enormous dark glasses signals to him with a hand. Sanctis approaches out of curiosity. First he thinks that for one reason or another maybe Elena has sent this woman to pick him up. Then—and more likely—that this woman, who's a stranger to him, has mistaken him for someone else.

But smiling at him and opening the car door with a quick movement, the woman gives a familiar "Hello" and invites him to climb in. Before Sanctis can even place the phonograph record, his briefcase, and the menacing parcel on the back seat, the car starts up, and the woman says, "Sorry to have kept you waiting. Last-minute problems. You mind if we talk here in the car?"

Because, yes, sir, even if it sounds like a fairy tale, this elegant woman—who doesn't look a minute over thirty and, in spite of the way she's sitting and the car's dark interior, gives one a glimpse of a slim body, the tanned legs of a sportswoman, and the disquieting absence of a bra under her red sweater—is none other than little Elena Vaccaro of Liberal Arts, the magazine's business manager, she of the Dr. Scholl footgear and the scummy handbag that used to hang off her shoulder.

"No, no, not at all," says Sanctis, trying to recover from the knockout blow of those suntanned knees and the red sweater. And forthwith he turns his whole body to take her in from top to bottom, adding in the deep voice of a matinee idol, "You're looking so pretty. So young. So different. I barely recognized you."

But to our new movie hero's disappointment, Elena Vaccaro appears impervious to those flirtatious feelers.

She says not a word, but with all the seriousness of a formula-one driver she gives her full attention to the steering wheel. She turns into a side street and seems to be heading straight for that part of Belgrano that slopes down to the river, but all at once, for no reason, she veers around one corner and then the next, and Sanctis notes that they're passing a point they were at only a minute ago. He also notes—and the detail doesn't fail to amuse him—that Elena keeps lifting her eyes to look through the rearview mirror.

It would be overstating it to say Sanctis is intrigued. But he is beside himself with amusement. He sits back comfortably, as if he were in front of his television, and waits. Let's see what she comes up with this time, he thinks—FBI agents, the KGB, emissaries of the Shah of Iran, or invaders from outer space. At any rate, riding around in a Renault 4L down dark little Belgrano side streets in the company of a beautiful woman, a braless brunette, can't be a bad thing. So, like a cat, Francisco Sanctis studies Elena Vaccaro while mapping out some infallible move.

But as if cottoning on to his lewd thoughts, Elena says suddenly, "I'm married. You?"

"Me too. With three kids. Only one, really—the others are my wife's, but actually it's as if they're my own," he replies, desperately aware that the conversation's becoming as erotic, dangerous, and suggestive as that of a couple of Rotarians in a cardiologist's waiting room.

"I haven't any," says Elena, continuing on the same high-minded, moral plane. "I've lived abroad awhile.

Central America, the United States—all over. To do with my husband's work, you know."

Still, the odd intonation she gave the word "husband" revives Sanctis's hopes. Elena pauses a long pause. Then, without any seeming relevance, she adds, "I lost contact with the whole gang from back then. You've probably kept up with them, I imagine."

"No, actually I haven't. My job doesn't leave me a lot of free time. It's a good job, this one, but I've been through some rough times," says Sanctis, quite ready as a last resort to pour out his life story in order to enter into some degree of intimacy. "Let me tell you, it's only this past year, really, that things have started taking off for me. I have—"

"Uh-huh," says Elena, not listening to the thrilling story of his life and punctuating his sentence in the middle. "Neither of us has much time, isn't that right? So we may as well get right down to brass tacks."

Sanctis notes that she hasn't called him Leonardo Medina again—not even once. "Well, as a matter of fact, I was waiting for you—I mean, as the thing seemed to be so urgent . . ." he says wickedly, pulling her leg.

"It is urgent." She cuts him short again.

The Renault never stops circling and circling, crossing Belgrano from one end to the other. Sometimes it gets as far as Colegiales, six or eight blocks south, sometimes as far as Núñez, six or eight north, but it always returns to the residential area of small dark streets that fall away toward the river. Her eyes fixed straight before her, Elena lets up on the accelerator and says without preamble, "Take down what I'm going to dictate. Two names and two addresses."

With studied deliberation, Sanctis draws his address book out of a pocket, moistens the tip of a pencil on his tongue, puts on the wily face of a private sleuth, and prepares to write out the names and addresses of the most famous and sinister secret agents to tread the western hemisphere these last fifty years.

Elena shoots him a sidelong glance and stops him. "No, come on now, not your address book. Any scrap of paper. Then learn it by heart and we'll get rid of the little piece of paper—all right?"

"Understood, Sergeant Pepper," Sanctis answers, stiff fingers up to an imaginary cap. He rummages in his wallet and comes across the crumpled receipt from a firm of opticians. Smoothing it out with the back of his hand, he lays it on the same wallet, and says, "I await your orders, Madame."

Not a word of reproach out of Elena Vaccaro, not even the expected sharp look to tell him cut the crapping around. Only her deliberate, level voice slowly dictating two names and two addresses.

"Julio Cardini. And the street—Álvarez Thomas 2837, third floor, apartment C. Bernardo Lipstein. Lacarra 4225. Got all that?"

"If you'd gone a bit slower I'd have managed something better than these hieroglyphics. But never mind, it's done."

"Fine, Sanctis. Now try to memorize it."

"Hey, look. Is this really necessary?" Sanctis asks,

somewhat fed up now. What with eight hours checking statements and poring over ledgers, he isn't exactly in the mood for little mnemonic games. "Anyhow, I'll memorize it later. Don't worry."

But insofar as famous, sinister secret agents are concerned Elena doesn't take kindly to procrastination.

"Better now. I won't bother you; you concentrate. Go ahead." And she keeps silent, hands on the steering wheel and eyes straight ahead, waiting for her order to be carried out to the letter.

Sanctis reluctantly dons his glasses, holds the slip of paper up to the dashboard, and puzzles out the handwriting—made shaky by the movement of the car—in which he has just scrawled.

He studies his lesson diligently, thinking, The Venezuelan magazine—nothing, not even the slightest mention. Sure, because it was only another stupid pretext. All too predictable, of course, but he's put out that Elena hasn't bothered even to apologize or at least offer an explanation.

In his mind he runs over the two names and addresses. He has them down cold, letter perfect. "Okay, ready," he says at last, with a weary sigh yet also with a trace of satisfaction for having done his duty.

"Repeat them for me, will you?"

In the voice of a schoolboy reciting, Sanctis repeats them.

"Good, now give me the piece of paper."

Sanctis turns over the optician's receipt, has a look at the date on it to make sure it's no longer worth a damn, and hands it to her. Still driving, Elena searches her handbag for a lighter and sets the paper afire. To do so, she has to hold it with the hand that's on the steering wheel, wait for the flame, then transfer it to her free hand. The operation is a bit tricky, and Sanctis reasons that it would have been easier to let him burn it. But obviously Elena has her own way of doing things.

For an instant or two the burning paper lights up Elena's face. In spite of the fact that it's now completely dark, she has not taken off her dark glasses. Her face is bony to the point of emaciation, and it's hard to recognize in it the Elenita Vaccaro of seventeen years back. Sanctis observes her closely and draws some hasty conclusions: solid economic background, a social life, a pitiless diet consisting of a small glass of grapefruit juice and such for breakfast, dance or body expression, swimming or tennis, beauty treatments and yoga, a very busy husband, independence, the odd lighthearted affair . . .

Well, despite the burnt offering and the sinister secret agents who are no doubt in hot pursuit of her right now by land and by sea, things aren't looking that bad, really.

Between her fingers Elena reduces the charred remains, the terrible ·damning evidence, and scatters the ash out the window. She drives on for several blocks and finally stops along a tree-lined street that Sanctis is unable to recognize. With a slightly theatrical gesture, she whips off her dark glasses, saying, "They're coming for them tonight."

She turns her head for the first time, fixing Sanctis

with her beautiful eyes, which are impeccably made up with pencil and brush, as if awaiting his reaction.

Sanctis begins to smell a rat. Sure, he says to himself, with everything that's going on in the country, is there any way Elenita's going to miss an opportunity to construct her own little horror film? Not on your life. Nevertheless, he decides he'll play dumb.

"You don't say. And who exactly is coming for them?"

Elena has a moment's hesitation. Maybe her intelligence headquarters in Casablanca isn't letting their agent 007 be more explicit. She shuts her eyes, drops her head, at last makes the risky decision, and answers in a low voice, "Air Force Intelligence." Then quickly changing her tone, she adds, "And please don't ask me anything else."

Oh, no, my dear, thinks Sanctis, full of indignation, you've no right. Playing policewoman with these things is way beyond the limits. The business about the CIA agents, that can be excused, but shitting around with this—oh, no. You don't have to be any wizard to know what it means that some guy is going to be picked up by Air Force Intelligence.

It means kidnapping, it means torture, it means systematic beating and a corpse hidden somewhere or thrown out of an airplane. It means what's happening to thousands of these guys—maybe at this very moment. Shit no, this nut can't be allowed just to come and take advantage of a situation that's deplorable, and of massacred thousands of sorry bastards, in order to play at moviemaking. No, this one she's not going to get away with.

"But really now, it can't be all that serious. It must be a routine procedure. Probably just an inquiry," says Sanctis with the intention of writing *finis* to Elena's film right here, of pulling in the kite string of her wild imagination.

Elena smiles, and her smile—Sanctis feels this—has in it a tinge of bitter irony. Exhaling a lungful of cigarette smoke, she says curtly, "It's not probably just an inquiry. Of that, rest assured."

CHAPTER VI

About how Elena Vaccaro finally gives in (figuratively speaking), and Francisco Sanctis, without considering that tobacco, as everyone knows, leads to chronic bronchitis and pulmonary emphysema, resumes smoking

Maybe it was Elena's smile. An ironic smile, agreed, but at the same time a tired smile—more than tired: weary. Maybe the way she said, "Of that, rest assured," or the slight movement of her head as she said it. Maybe the plainness and even restraint of her words, so unlike the voluble, full-range dramatics of old—it's as if he's hearing her—when she was being pursued by secret agents and evil international conspiracies with headquarters out where she lived in Ciudadela. Just an intuitive flash, a sudden illumination. But Sanctis senses that this time Elena is not inventing, that her anguish is genuine, that the imminent death of these two guys has to be genuine, that in some mysterious way she has genuinely found all this out and is looking—perhaps ineptly—for someone to tell it to.

But this conviction or, to be more exact, intuition that

Elena is speaking the truth, rather than making conversation easier is making it harder. Sanctis now knows that even if he wanted to, he could no longer poke fun at her in the lighthearted way he was doing only a while ago, calling her Sergeant Pepper or Wonder Woman or other clownish things of the sort. He also knows—Elena requested it of him quite clearly—that it's better to ask no questions. Therefore, he's not sure what to say.

For a time he remains silent, acting as if he were mulling over Elena's words. In fact, he's thinking about how to respond, about what words will be the right ones to fill this uncomfortable silence which has already gone on too long. In the end he comes up with something that, as soon as he gets it out, strikes him as the stupidest utterance in the world.

"These things are terrible, really."

And he falls back into his witless silence.

As a matter of fact, he's waiting. Waiting for what? Well, in the first place, for Elena to relinquish another bit of information so that he can verify his hunch that this time she's not lying. In the second place, and more important, to find out why. Why of all people did she telephone him?

But Elena keeps staring at him, and seemingly she has no intention of adding a word to anything she's said. To relax the tension, to shift the emphasis and bring the conversation around to a more familiar and less difficult terrain, Sanctis says, "Should I tell you the truth, Elena?

I never really bought it about the Venezuelan magazine. It seemed to me a pretext or something."

He notices that he's greedily inhaling the smoke of a king-size Imparcial. His first in four months. He cannot remember exactly when he lit it.

"Yes. Yes, of course, it was a pretext," Elena answers, with the same sad smile of a while earlier.

As this doesn't really clarify anything, Sanctis presses on. "You say a pretext, but a pretext for what? So we could meet? So you could tell me what you just told me? It's so odd. And why a Venezuelan magazine?"

"So we could meet, that goes without saying. I don't know—it was the first thing that came into my head," says Elena, not even apologizing for the bald lie, and she falls back into silence, as if waiting for Sanctis to speak, for him to take the first step.

But what step can Sanctis actually take? It's not as though he sought any of this or asked her to share the dangerous information with him. So he, too, shelters behind a silence that has about it a touch of impoliteness and stubbornness. He feels tense, ill at ease. From somewhere or other an unfocused, not altogether explicable fear circles round him.

Elena has no recourse but to speak. She seems at first to be trying to put her words together very carefully, to say no more than is absolutely necessary. But later, in spite of her attempt at control, Sanctis feels a slight quaver of emotion behind her sentences.

"Listen carefully, Sanctis," she says. "Whether or not

you know these people doesn't interest me. Nor am I interested in whether you know anyone who can get into contact with them. But they've got to be warned, don't you understand that? They can be saved."

Yes, of course, it seems to be a question of saving the lives of these two guys. But what can he do? And what's any of this got to do with him, after all? Sanctis mumbles something hurried and unclear about his being completely out of touch with people of that kind. He explains that he hasn't even the faintest notion where you'd start in a case like this. He is about to mention his plans for that night, but Elena interrupts him with a wave of the hand. Her fingertips nearly touch Sanctis's lips, as if asking him to keep silent. And Sanctis keeps silent.

"Please, don't say anything," Elena tells him. "I gave you a piece of information, nothing else. You know what you can or can't do."

But Sanctis has no intention, particularly in a situation like the present one, of letting Elena form any false ideas about his cleverness or his secret contacts or, simply, his courage.

"Look here, Elena," he says, making an effort to be honest, "I don't think there's a lot I can do. I admit it. I mean, I don't think I can do anything—what's the point of misleading you? I'm going to give it some thought, though, and I'll talk to you about it later. Look for another way—that's what I'm really telling you."

"There's something I want to bring up about that too," says Elena, looking at her watch and starting the

Renault. "You aren't going to have another chance to talk to me. We're never going to see each other again. And I don't have to say you're going to forget all about this meeting, do I? Come what may, no matter what, you're not going to tell a soul where this information came from. This has to be absolutely clear, and no doubt you understand why."

So she hasn't the remotest idea of clarifying anything. And just like that, she drops the bundle in his lap, bye-bye, and she's off.

"Yes, yes, I understand why. I understand perfectly why," he says in as cutting a way as possible. "You don't want to get involved. All right. That's beautifully plain. But, my friend, there are too many things about this that aren't exactly crystal-clear."

Elena appears not to have been listening. The car drives along Libertador to Guayra, then turns up Guayra to Cabildo.

"I'll drop you off at Monroe, all right?"

"Sure, sure. That's fine," Sanctis says dryly, not wanting to talk anymore and not bothering to hide his displeasure.

Elena acknowledges his anger. She slows the car down a bit, and in a voice that tries to sound maternal or indulgent, she says at last, "What is it you don't understand, then? Let's see."

"Well, hardly anything, really. Why did you pick me, for example?"

"Okay. I'll tell you why."

She ponders it for several seconds, but as she is obviously calculating that the bare minute left before reaching Monroe won't be enough for all she has to disclose, she passes right by the street without stopping, continues along to Pampa, and turns left again toward the river.

Now Elena speaks quickly and easily. Her explanation, though apparently farfetched, is basically believable. At least, Sanctis feels inclined to believe her—in spite of his initial mistrust.

Not very long after the business of their magazine and their marches, Elena tells him, she happened to get married. (She doesn't mention her husband's name or occupation.) She lived abroad for a while. It appears she has done a lot of traveling. From the time she returned to Buenos Aires—that was two years ago—she never got in touch with any of the old crowd. "I live," she says, "shut away in a world I'd rather not talk about." But she does suggest that she can't find in this world "a single person worthy of trust."

Yes, as a matter of fact, all quite believable. That world she'd rather not talk about could be anything—promiscuous sex, the jet set, close encounters of a third kind, or stamp collecting—and it really does not interest him. This is why Sanctis won't ask her anything about it. But it still isn't clear why exactly he and not any of the other twenty or thirty roughnecks of that time was chosen as the recipient of this nice little gift. And, of course, this he does ask her.

"No reason," Elena answers cleverly, shrugging her shoulders. "Sheer chance. And also lack of time. I had to pick someone, and just one person. I only got wind of the thing at five o'clock, so you can imagine."

"Imagine what?" asks Sanctis.

"Well . . . suddenly I thought of you. I always considered you an upright sort, someone I could trust and . . . well, trust for something like this, I mean. Naturally, I also thought that as you are the way you are, a fighter, a rebel, maybe you were in touch with some group—" She realizes she's put her foot in it and quickly tries to wriggle out. "I don't know, I just figured that you'd know how, that you'd manage to find some way." Her scientific explanation concluded, by way of a brilliant summing up she adds, "In a word, I played this card as I might have played any other, you get me?" Pause, and again the shrug of the shoulders. "Well, anyway, it's over now, and there's nothing else I can do. Call it a problem of conscience if you like."

He still wants to know how she managed to get his telephone number at work (in about five minutes' time, according to Sanctis's calculations) and locate him so quickly. But before he can even ask, Elena explains. She mentions a certain Oyarzábal, an ex-member of their magazine and now head of a publishing empire specializing in women's magazines and other such glossy trivia, a sort of tycoon of commercial journalism, for whom, according to Elena, it was no trouble to find Sanctis's number. So, then, Oyarzábal gave her Luchini & Monsreal's number. Simple as that.

Sanctis recalls that he has bumped into Oyarzábal at the old London Bar three or four times—and always by

49

chance. On one of those occasions, as a mere formality, they had exchanged phone numbers.

So at least this part of the story seemed believable. There are still a few obscure points, but it's obvious that Elena is not going to give in and reveal any more. Besides, Sanctis has the feeling that his curiosity may prove irritating—not part of the program, let's say—or even suspicious should the case be that dizzy Elena really is involved in something unusual. So he decides to hold back the half-dozen questions still running around upstairs and for the time being not rock the boat. Lowering his head as if judiciously weighing up matters, he murmurs an "Aha" whose meaning he himself does not understand.

Nevertheless, he needs explained one aspect of the thing that touches on him: what specifically he's expected to do. With a certain hesitation, then, he asks something that sounds stupid but that, okay, he's going to have to ask sooner or later.

"They'd have to be seen personally, I suppose."

"Yes," answers Elena, "but it would be a lot better if it weren't by you. Some organization would be preferable. What can I say? Someone who didn't know you, let alone me." She pauses briefly to stub out a cigarette in the ashtray, adding, "As you probably realize, this could be dangerous."

Sanctis, who had not altogether realized that any danger might be involved, and in spite of his intention to ask no questions, lets slip a spontaneous "In what way?"

The joyride on the Belgrano-Núñez-Saavedra-Colegiales merry-go-round has therefore to be extended a few more turns. Because at the last moment Elena decides suddenly to be a bit more explicit. Maybe she senses Sanctis's total lack of experience in matters of this kind. (Her unwarranted supposition is that he's mixed up with some subversive group.) Maybe she's afraid that this honest but not very bright guy—for such is her assessment of the present-day Francisco Sanctis— is biting off more than he can chew without clearly knowing what he's risking. Possibly she figures that she must make some kind of confession if she wants to win his complete trust. Possibly she's letting herself be carried away by her own words and the climate of intimacy born there in the darkness of the car and aided by cigarettes, words spoken in low voices, and a faceless dread. Possibly, as well, the confession has simply slipped out and later on she'll regret what she said. The fact is that Elena stops the Renault again—this time on Olleros near Luis María Campos—takes the Imparcial that Sanctis offers her (he's helping himself to his third), rests a hand on Sanctis's arm, which she hasn't done before, and tells him almost sweetly, "Listen here, Sanctis, one shouldn't overlook the possibility that this whole thing's a trap."

Great. Just what he needed. Sanctis's mouth literally hangs open. Suspecting that the little he believes he's understood he's understood badly, he asks in irritation, "Hey, explain right now what you mean, do you mind?"

"Yes, a trap, an ambush for me or my husband," Elena replies. "That's what I want to tell you—maybe this in-

51

formation has been passed on to us to see if we make a wrong move. That's why I can't go personally, you see? That's why I'm asking you to get in touch with some organization. People like that know what to do."

"But what's your husband got to do with this song-and-dance?" says Sanctis like a betrayed lover.

Again the silence. Again Elena's manner that borders on the theatrical, as if she's undergoing some terrible inner struggle. At last, without looking at him, she answers, "He's an Air Force officer."

She said it in a barely audible voice, and Sanctis feels he may not have heard properly. "What did you say?"

"I said he's an Air Force officer. That's where it all stems from. You beginning to get the picture now? But he has nothing to do with this—I want that clear. I only found out by accident, and it occurred to me to try to do something."

Well, isn't this all very cozy? Elena calls this piece of tomfoolery she's just set in motion doing something. Telephoning him, arranging a meeting, burning to let him in on a scrap of gossip she's picked up by accident, as if he were that Sandler making a fuss in the Congress a couple of years ago about these kidnappings, or the Secretary-General of the UN, or Christ knows what. Sanctis is on the brink of losing all patience.

"Listen to me, toots. This is what you call doing something?"

"Well, sure. It's doing something. What else was there? I already told you your name turned up the way anyone else's could have." The words don't strike him as very felicitous at the moment, which may be why Elena makes an attempt to sugar the pill. "But now I'm really glad it was you. You know, you haven't changed much," she tells him, smiling, her hand on Sanctis's hand.

"You say I haven't changed much, but I have. Oh, if I could just begin to tell you . . ." says Sanctis, about to launch into a solid explanation of why he's not the right guy for this sort of job. But Elena cuts him short.

"You remember the names?"

Sanctis postpones his explanation and once more repeats his lesson: "Julio Cardini, Álvarez Thomas 2837, third floor, apartment C. Bernardo Lipstein, Lacarra 4225."

"They usually come for them in the early hours. Three or four in the morning. So there's still plenty of time to do something," says Elena as if it were a piece of cake. "And now, really, I've got to go. I'm sorry, but it's better if you get off here."

They are near the corner of Olleros and Luis María Campos, over twenty blocks from his home. But Elena's decision seems irrevocable.

While he feels around on the back seat for his briefcase, the phonograph record, and the parcel, he has a brilliant idea, and he mentions it.

"You don't know their phone numbers?"

"What phone numbers?"

"Well . . . these people's. Maybe they could be reached by telephone—what do you think?"

Elena starts the motor. Giving him a peck on the cheek, and as if she were addressing a slightly retarded child, she answers, "My dear, do you think if these two had telephones I'd have called you?"

Sanctis is aware of having said something very foolish. The second or hundredth foolish thing that evening. He doesn't want to open the door and say goodbye to Elena just like this. He would still like to tell her that what she has just done is meaningless, that he undoubtedly will do nothing of what she expects, that the two guys will be bagged like a couple of pigeons that very night, that having picked him to pass on the information to was a mistake, a silly move, that maybe there's still time for her to find someone else, someone more . . .

Elena hurries him. "I'm late, really."

Sanctis has no other choice than to get out of the car cluttered with all that's still buzzing around in his head and with all his bothersome impedimenta, clutching these as best he can.

Elena shuts the car door after him, dons her dark glasses again, smiles, and as the car starts up waves her hand.

Standing at the curb on Olleros, Sanctis awkwardly waves back with the hand that's gripping his briefcase. He sees the Renault reach Luis María Campos and turn at high speed toward Palermo.

CHAPTER VII

In which, under the beneficent emanations of María Angélica and of a spur-of-the-moment ham-and-cheese special, Sanctis utters a line worthy of Henri Bergson—that is to say

That this, in fact, is where the real story of Francisco Sanctis begins. That story which was announced (the reader having been duly cautioned) at the outset of this little book; a story which for better or worse must justify each of these painstaking pages and to which everything related so far is mere prologue.

Because it just happens that it's right here in this short, unusually dark stretch of Olleros Street (it was not for nothing that the prudent Elena Vaccaro chose this spot to park her Renault), following the muddled meeting we know all about, that we find Francisco Sanctis alone for the first time. That is, alone with his own muddle.

Let's begin by admitting that the place where Elena has landed him is a bit odd. Flanked by a towering wall, cracked and patchy and sprouting moss, yet dominated and dwarfed by an enormous acacia—its roots lift and split a number of the tiles that pave the sidewalk, its head almost totally obscures the bluish light of a street lamp—the fact is that this piece of walkway has about it a touch of gloom and ghostliness. Here, anyway, neglected and untamed, the spot seems at first sight to have nothing in common with the rest of the street, with its pretty bungalows and small private homes.

But ghostly or not, the spot in itself does not justify this state bordering on the unreal—let's call it that straightaway—that has come over Sanctis and that makes him suspect that everything he has lived in the last minutes has been a kind of dream. A dream from which he hasn't yet awakened, since it seems to linger on in this overpowering wall, in these huge cracks, in these paving tiles that ride one on the other obscenely, in a darkness totally beyond municipal regulations.

Perhaps this is why, owing to the nasty sensation of being almost on a visit from another world, nothing better occurs to him than to stand there like a fool, studying the acacia's furrowed trunk, the wide, mustachioed cracks in the wall, the letters, white on a blue background, of an unexpected street sign. Perhaps this is also why he moves out under the street lamp, his steps hesitant, to see what time it is. Basic technique, all of it, but guaranteed effective for plugging into a reality that keeps trying to slip through one's fingers like sand.

He's surprised to learn that it's only twenty-five minutes to ten. He thought it was a lot later. Actually, he has no clear idea of the time that passed between Elena's appearance at the corner of Cabildo and Juramento and her giddy disappearance along Luis María Campos. The words "appearance" and "disappearance" are his own, and they cause him to chuckle. "Shit, as though she were a ghost," he says to himself.

Now, as by degrees he begins connecting with reality, he has the feeling of having been thrust into a time outside time, into an interlude of daydreams and preposterousness, with addresses learned by heart, bits of paper burned to ash, vague husbands serving in Air Force Intelligence, bureaucratically planned kidnappings for three or maybe four in the morning, and mysterious informers who practice yoga and body expression. An interlude during which not he but another Francisco Sanctis, much more adrift, naive, and susceptible to bamboozling than the present Sanctis or the one who at five that afternoon received a telephone call at Luchini & Monsreal, would have committed an endless series of blunders, acting exactly the way one acts in dreams, accepting without question and as perfectly normal the most unparalleled facts and details—a toothbrush that's also an aunt; a fish that slips off a hook, makes its way across a room, and utters threats in the voice of Father Cioppi; a four-eyed roly-poly girl who's also an absolutely stunning dish; an optician's receipt that must pass through ritual fire; a pair who will be brought in by a goon squad this very night.

The matter deserves at least a half-dozen deep breaths and several minutes of calm meditation.

Slowly, he starts walking toward Cabildo. He would like to do the whole twenty-odd blocks home on foot. He knows it would be a good way of ordering his mind. He would like to remember as much as humanly possible of each of the events that took place between twenty-five to nine and twenty-five to ten and try to understand them; to try as well to understand his own behavior, which strikes him now as a sampling of random replies and sheer rubbish. But above all to recall everything Elena said, and there on the wide, well-lit sidewalk of Cabildo, far from her enticing red sweater, to separate intelligently the wheat from the chaff, the truth from that irresponsible tomfoolery that was part and parcel of the Elenita Vaccaro of old.

But he also knows it will be impossible for him to think with even an iota of serenity while his hands are ignominiously busy with a phonograph record, a briefcase, and a package that threatens disaster at any moment.

So? So the best thing would be to plop himself down in the first bar he comes to, and there, calmly seated, carry out his program of meditation.

A bar, as everyone knows, is usually the best remedy for temporary sensations of unreality or other lunacies. Tables, windows, chairs, the predictable Spanishness of the waiter, the bottles of Chissotti and Anís Ocho Hermanos behind the counter, are elements that, because they are familiar, because they have been witnesses to and accomplices in hundreds of past lunacies, tie one to reality with solid bonds, however wild and slippery reality may become. This, on the whole, is what Sanctis must be thinking as he reaches Cabildo, and that's why, instead of looking around there for a café or a bar, he crosses the avenue, setting out for a small place he knows at the corner of Ciudad de la Paz and Lacroze. Here, where he hasn't put a foot in years, he once sat and copied out orders when he worked as a salesman, and on several occasions when he was fired from a job he came here just to curse his rotten luck and the shitty world that wasn't making room for him. All in the past, of course, but Sanctis believes that this filthy hole-in-the-wall will help him find the way he seems to have lost and, at the same time, transform this appalling shambles he has in his hand into a parcel worthy of the name.

With his package miraculously still in one piece and dangling from his hand like a trapeze, he is crossing the worn-thin threshold of the bar when, for no particular reason, as if he were routinely obeying an order, he finds himself going over in his head the two names and two addresses. He remembers them perfectly, and this sets off in him two quite contradictory feelings. On the one hand, that even in these confused circumstances his brain is functioning properly; this pleases him and gives him a touch of pride. On the other, that these names and addresses imprinted on his memory are an obligation of sorts, a nagging presence that he doesn't know what to do with and of which, in his heart of hearts, he'd like to be rid as soon as possible. A nuisance much like the package of canned goods whose coarse twine, forever on the verge of coming undone, keeps cutting into his flesh, son of a bitch, and of which it's also becoming urgently necessary to be rid. With the slight difference that the moment he arrives home he'll fling the package aside, but these names and addresses—what's he to do with them? Where in Christ's name is he going to fling them?

He comes to the conclusion that these names and addresses are proof—almost tangible, almost physical— that all that's just taken place inside the partly lit, circling Renault was no dream. And this puts him in mind of those stories of apparitions that from time to time are bandied about Buenos Aires. In them, some object—a dagger, a scarf, a woman's dress—suddenly materializes, the bizarre remains of a fantastic incident, of a nightmare. And then, confronted with the inexplicable appearance of these items, one comes to question whether the nightmare really was a nightmare.

The damning evidence, the humiliating presence of the nightmare in the world of real things, is that little series of words and numbers: juliocardini álvarezthomas twenty-eight thirty-seven three c bernardolipstein lacarra forty-two twenty-five. A presence which prevents Francisco Sanctis from saying, as he would like to, that it was all just a dream or a brief attack of acute elenitis stimulated by the dark and the red sweater; throw a hygienic spadeful of earth over the matter and go back home untroubled.

He is surprised by a gruff Spanish voice asking what he would like (Sanctis hadn't realized he was sitting at a small table next to the window), and he quickly answers, "A ham-and-cheese special and a Coke."

He smiles to himself, wondering through how many twists and turns of his memory those words had to travel to come out whole on his lips this way—from a bar at the corner of Córdoba and Pasteur twenty years ago to this hole in the wall on Ciudad de la Paz. And he asks himself whether this funny leap back has some pointed meaning. Has it, for example, anything to do with the resurrection of that buried Francisco Sanctis, the "fighter and rebel" of Elenita Vaccaro's decidedly myopic vision—however much she tries to disguise it now with contact lenses?

He shakes his head from side to side, telling himself that as long as he's alone, even with the supposed intention of putting his ideas in order, a good many more stupid things are going to find their way into his mind. At this point he admits that the notion of working things out on his own is obviously not leading anywhere, that this time, as so often in the past, he has urgent need of María Angélica.

But while all his efforts are concentrated on the damned parcel, repacking and doing it up anew, he suddenly remembers the Crespis. Maybe they're already there waiting for me, he says to himself, thinking that if they really intended dropping in that night it would be a royal foul-up. That that night he'd prefer having some time alone with María Angélica, talking to her, maybe asking her advice. María Angélica—sensible, sweet, motherly, and understanding. María Angélica with her prematurely graying hair and her candid, girlish face. María Angélica, with whom he's in the habit of talking over almost everything—everything from his back pains to the best schools for the kids or color for a new suit. How is it he hadn't thought of her until now?

Suddenly he reconsiders, aware that this time—and for fairly obvious reasons—he can't really tell María Angélica about what's going on. And this impossibility, forced on him in part by Elena, yes, but even more by a worry for his own safety, weighs him down with a sense of helplessness.

To be unable even to discuss the matter with María Angélica makes it seem more difficult, more confused, more dangerous. Having to tackle a problem of this kind alone, he admits, is not at all to his liking.

But on second thought, is it really necessary to keep anything from a person as solidly reliable as María Angélica? Well, no need to exaggerate, he thinks, trying to steel himself; maybe he'll find a way to broach the subject in—what?—a roundabout way, an intimating way. Not a word about Elena Vaccaro, of course, or Julio Cardini or Bernardo Lipstein—or frigging Air Force Intelligence. Instead, he might be able to skirt the issue, saying for example that someone came to him with the story. Or maybe a general approach would be better. Talk about what's going on in the country, how from one moment to the next one can find oneself involved in something without really having anything to do with it. Well, something like that. He is sure that María Angélica, who's always been clearheaded, simple, and straightforward, who always has her feet on the ground, will provide him with that one right word, that suggestion, that piece of advice he so desperately needs. But even if she doesn't, even if María Angélica can't come up with the solution he is after, the mere fact of talking to her—this he knows from experience—will give the problem a dimension both human and understandable. Things will stop being phantasmagoric, senseless, and become subject matter for conversation, for a civilized exchange of ideas far more productive—of this he has no doubt—than the awful carnival course spinning round in his head at breakneck speed and threatening, as long as he keeps everything to himself, to accelerate more and more, turning into a vortex, frantic and out of control.

He gets up now, makes his way to the telephone, and dials his home number. The Crespis, he learns, will not be coming. Fernando rang to say their younger boy had a temperature too, and they were putting off the visit for another night. Thank God, thinks Sanctis, and he tells María Angélica he'll be there in a little while. Remarkable. He feels better, calmer. Returning to the table, he wolfs down his ham-and-cheese special.

Speaking to María Angélica, even for this bare minute, seems to have had a healthy effect on him, and—a kind of sudden lucidity coming over him—Sanctis decides to weigh the facts. It doesn't matter whether he resolves anything now; at least he'll come to María Angélica with an intelligently thought-out problem and not this barrel of monkeys he himself can't seem to get a grip on.

We shouldn't allow ourselves to be carried away by impulse but should see things as they are, he says to himself, and he's at the point of clearing his throat—as if having just delivered the pithiest statement of the century. Taking a sip of Coca-Cola, he continues. First off, who is Elena Vaccaro? Answer: Elena Vaccaro is a phony middle-class number who, to appease a surely rotten conscience, approaches someone she doesn't know, inviting him very sweetly to do something that she, by her own confession, does not dare do. Why doesn't she dare? Because it's possible the whole thing's a trap.

63

All right, those are the facts. Now, what's the best way of responding to these facts? Does one ignore the danger lurking in the shadows, gratefully accepting the invitation as if it were no more than an invitation to a picnic or a hand of canasta? No, sir; not on your life. Why not? Well, because among a number of other weighty reasons, one just isn't all that dumb.

So far so good. But in actuality the question has another side, he tells himself, as though he were laying out the facts in the columns of a ledger. That other side is the following. Inserting an imaginary colon, he adds: Middle-class or not, candidate chosen at random or not, it's plain that these two guys will be beaten to a pulp. That is to say, maybe there's some way of warning them—if and when one came up with the courage to wade into such a mess. That is to say that in this case, in addition to screwing up these sons of a thousand bitches of Air Force Intelligence (which is always a pretty good thing), one could save the skins of these two poor bastards. That is to say . . .

That is to say that his newfound analytical ability is already cracking under what seems to be the vanguard of a new and multitudinous round of mental chaos.

That is to say that with the desperate gesture of a shipwrecked sailor, Francisco Sanctis waves his arm to call the waiter.

He pays, loads up briefcase, record, and remade package, looks for a taxi, and rushes pell-mell to the one person who may be able to put some order to this metaphorical carnival ride—María Angélica.

CHAPTER VIII

In which the heady aphrodisiac qualities of Zen Buddhism, mixed in the correct proportion with a certain French perfume and a nice bottle of Suter (chilled, as white wine should be), are upheld

It's a bit after twenty past ten when at last Sanctis turns the key in his apartment door.

Hearing him, María Angélica rushes to the hall, book in hand, glasses thrust up on her forehead. This signals that the children are in bed, the kitchen's been cleaned, and Spot, who's barking wildly from the balcony, is back after his evening stroll. In other words, the conditions indispensable to a private, peaceful conversation with María Angélica have miraculously been granted.

But still, even if things are turning out as one would have wished (the timely flu of the younger of the Crespis must have been an act of Sanctis's guardian angel), Sanctis knows he must keep a grip on himself, at least for the time being, and come up with the exact yet offhand way of launching into the subject without letting out of the bag what's already taken place that night—to say nothing of the inner conflict that right now is eating away at him a lot more than he would have believed possible only a while ago.

Because, he warns himself, it's no good bursting in and latching on to María Angélica like some shipwrecked sailor and then naively shooting his bolt, thereby revealing all too clearly the seriousness of his private dilemma. If he were to carry on that way, not holding back as he should but immediately wading in—however much he'd beat around the bush, employ diversionary tactics, and adopt a conversational tone—María Angélica would immediately smell a rat. Her radar would be working, she'd ask questions, and in no time at all— of this he has no doubt—his carefully planned strategy to safeguard his secret (the secret of Elena Vaccaro, of the Renault 4L, of the names Julio Cardini and Bernardo Lipstein, meticulously tucked away in some fold of his memory) would go straight out the window in the face of María Angélica's maternal look and her pointed, straightforward questions, which, he also knows, it would be impossible for him not to answer.

So Sanctis begins by imprinting a tender kiss on María Angélica's cheek, then drops the record, his briefcase, and the package on the nearest armchair, and artfully addresses himself to the problem of how to consult the oracle (which in fact is what he pretends he's doing) without the oracle's realizing what he's consulting her about.

A hard thing to do. A lot harder—he now sees this clearly—than he'd supposed when, seated comfortably at a table in a bar, out of María Angélica's domain, he'd planned this operation. Because María Angélica pays less attention to one's words than to one's tone of voice, one's pauses, and Christ knows what other subtle, uncontrollable details, and—he knows from experience—to play around with that sixth sense of hers is like trying to make yourself invisible in front of an X-ray machine.

In pursuance of the first part of his plan, then, Sanctis sinks down on the sofa, stretches, yawns noisily, and, trying to put on an air of nonchalance, he asks about the kids and about the book María Angélica is reading.

Completely exhausted by football and swimming, the kids conked out right after supper. The book's the one Elisa Crespi lent her that afternoon, and it's about Zen Buddhism. Elisa considers it wonderful, but María Angélica finds it somewhat boring. The plumber didn't show up again, service charges on the apartment have doubled, Marty got a hundred in math, and Perugia phoned at around nine o'clock. "You want to eat something?"

Sanctis says no, he's just had a sandwich on the way home and he's not hungry.

"You look tired. You must get to bed early tonight," says María Angélica, looking at him over her glasses. She's sitting in an armchair beside a lamp. Her book is open, but she hasn't made up her mind yet whether to go on with her Zen Buddhism.

"Yes, I am a bit tired. Had an awful day today," says Sanctis, massaging his face.

He sneaks a look at his watch. Quarter to eleven. Shit, time flies, and he can't find the way to start up the conversation. Several possibilities he dismisses out of hand, considering them either farfetched or too obvious or just plain dumb. At long last, since his imagination—being slow or stuck—seems not to want to come to his aid, he says something that still strikes him as dumb and at the same time farfetched, but at this hour it's all his weary brain can come up with. Staring at the blank television screen, perhaps trying to pretend he's speaking about something he's seen there, he suddenly says, "Tell me, María Angélica. Supposing just like that, completely out of the blue, you're given the chance to save some guy's life—"

"What guy?" María Angélica swiftly cuts in, for in most cases she hates this kind of abstract talk.

"Well, never mind what guy. Any guy—period. Someone you don't know," says Sanctis, trying to play the annoyed husband.

"Something to do with politics?" says María Angélica, more as a statement than a question, again stopping the ball dead and venturing into territory where Sanctis doesn't want her.

Caught offside, for a moment or two Sanctis hesitates.

"All right, it may have something to do with politics. Why not?" he answers at last, almost at a loss and already regretting having not flatly denied it, since for the thousandth time he realizes how difficult it is telling María Angélica even a white lie. His fear now is that simply by looking into his eyes María Angélica will discover not only his inner confusion but also the color of Elena Vaccaro's sweater and the number of cigarettes smoked in the semidarkness of the Renault. Having put his foot in it, he now tries to set matters straight, adding, "But it could be something else too. Say a criminal matter—why not? Actually that's not important. The point is that there's a guy who's going to be knocked off, and you can save his skin. That's it. What would you do?"

María Angélica thinks it over, trying to understand the meaning of this rather pointless rhetorical question. She imagines, not altogether sure, that this may be some sort of psychological test. She takes off her glasses, placing the book almost ceremoniously on an end table, shrugs her shoulders, and says in a perfectly natural way, "I'd save him." Another spell of silence, as if she were weighing her own words, her head teeters from side to side, and she repeats, "Yes, sir, I'd save him." And by way of justification, she adds, "You know I don't go along with crime, I don't care what quarter it comes from."

It's an answer. A clear, straightforward answer and so in keeping with María Angélica, as a matter of fact, that Sanctis pays close attention, records it, and temporarily files it away in a little compartment of his memory for later use. But for a definitive answer (for a definitive solution) surely the computer requires more information, and Sanctis hastens to gather it.

"All right. Now listen to me. Just suppose that by doing it—saving this guy's life, I mean—you're taking a risk. Let's say you're told it's dangerous, that it could be a trap or something."

María Angélica turns serious. This absurd conversation, unconnected with reality, puts her off, and she wants it to end at once. The way Sanctis is faltering makes her drop the idea of a psychological test, and for a minute she suspects her husband might be in some trouble. Deep down, she wishes Sanctis would make up his mind to speak clearly, because all this empty talk is beginning to bore her almost as much as Zen Buddhism does. Besides—to be frank about it—this is not what she had her heart set on tonight. After putting the children to bed, she'd bathed, perfumed herself, and put on some special lingerie, and what she had in mind was a much more satisfying and exciting program than this dull talk about traps, lives to be saved, and murders. In part to hurry things along (and so shorten the way to bed), but also out of an ingrained habit of clearing up ambiguities, she forces herself to answer candidly.

"I wouldn't get involved, you know," she says. "That's my opinion. I'm no heroine. It's not just the life of one person that's at stake."

She stretches a hand toward the table as if to pick up her reading glasses. But she changes her mind and drops it. Sinking down into the armchair, she frowns slightly, looks at Sanctis, and says, "But why are you asking all these silly questions? Can you please tell me?"

Sanctis feels suddenly naked, defenseless, cornered. However hard he tries, he sees no way out. Shrugging his shoulders, he stupidly answers, "Well . . . no reason, really. I just wanted to know."

The childishness of his answer is almost a confession.

Out of the corner of her eye María Angélica looks up at the ceiling as if imploring Saint Peter to grant her one more measure of patience. Then she sighs, stares at Sanctis, and comes straight to the point. "What's going on with you? Have you some problem? Come on, tell me, and cut out all this mystery."

Sanctis is one step away from a full confession, which he feels would bring him relief. He tells himself that, after all, he held on as long as he could, and that to speak honestly at this stage of the game now seems the only way open to him.

He wonders if he should begin with the appearance of Elena Vaccaro at the corner of Cabildo and Juramento or with the telephone call to the office, when suddenly a reaction sets in and he makes one last desperate attempt to evade María Angélica's question.

"Problems? Me? What problems can I have? Come on!" Again he falls back on the old stance of the annoyed spouse. But realizing that to resort to this worn-out ploy twice in the course of the same night may prove dangerous, he waves his hand about in a fairly ambiguous gesture and pretends he's agreeing to make things clear.

"Listen carefully," he says, trying to thread a way out of the minefield and bring the conversation around to a less loaded subject. "You think about these things from time to time. One sees the direction the country's going."

"Yes, darling, we all know the direction the country's going. But what's that got to do with what you asked me?"

It gets harder and harder for Sanctis to resist. Five minutes more conversing like this and he'll sing anything she asks. Still bravely holding his ground, he answers with a voice that's a touch schoolteacherish. "I asked the question because from one minute to the next, the way the country's headed, one can get mixed up in things—things one wasn't exactly looking for."

But it's no use trying to palm off meaningless answers on María Angélica. "What can you be involved in? Come on, tell me, because I'm in the dark."

"Well . . . I've been hearing about one or two cases. Just to give an example close to home, Monsreal's got a friend who had to keep a young couple hidden out at his place—imagine that. Army Intelligence was after them. So it was said. A question of life or death, think about that. Of course, they were more or less related, but the guy took a risk, no?"

Sanctis is desperate for a cigarette. But to light one now means he'd have to explain how and when he took up smoking again after quitting for four months. He settles for giving the hidden pack of Imparciales a little pat, then answers, "Well, to tell the truth, they aren't related. But more or less. Didn't you yourself tell me that the Fernándezes' oldest boy, Lucho, left home? Okay, suppose Lucho were to appear here one day and tell you—"

"Listen to me, darling," María Angélica cuts in, alarmed. "I don't know what's going on in your head. But pay attention—there's no possible way we could hide him out here. Just think of the children."

Good, thinks Sanctis, relieved. The diversionary tactic is working. Now María Angélica will concentrate all her firepower on that flank, and for the time being pressure will be relieved where he's really vulnerable. If he wants to stay out of danger there, he must beat a strategic retreat at once. At once because Julio Cardini and Bernardo Lipstein's names, which only moments ago seemed to him totally buried and invisible to María Angélica's eyes, he now feels pulsating in his mind like the little lights on a panel in a science fiction movie. So strong is this feeling that the two names are there clamoring for attention, he's afraid even a small slip on his part will allow María Angélica to read them clearly just by glancing at his face.

"Of course," he hastens to answer, "I mentioned the Fernándezes' kid, but I could have mentioned a few others. Don't imagine he's going to put in an appearance around here. Besides, who knows where he is. He may not even be in the country."

María Angélica isn't convinced by Sanctis's hasty withdrawal. Or so it appears. She says insistently, "You know how the military behave in these cases. They burst in like wild beasts, and they make no distinctions."

Sanctis keeps ceding ground. Willingly.

"That's right," he says. "They sweep up everybody. How can you hide some guy away in your house? Impossible. But you see? It's something one needs to have thought out beforehand, don't you agree? That's what I was trying to get at."

73

"Out of the question. Absolutely out of the question, anyone hiding out here," María Angélica insists again, just in case, leaning back in her armchair and addressing the wall opposite.

It's the right moment to get up and put an end to the conversation. So Sanctis nods approval and gets up. He takes a few steps about the living room, runs a hand over the backs of his phonograph records, which are neatly ordered on a shelf, softly whistles a Bach fugue, and looks out the window. He then points to the ominous package of canned goods there on the armchair and tells María Angélica that next time it would be better to buy more and he could have the delivery van drop it off. "Lugging all that along the streets—never again."

And with these words, so it seems, María Angélica's final misgivings are buried, for, having heard him out, she now dons her glasses and returns in peace to her boring Zen Buddhism.

Still, Sanctis is not altogether reassured. He wonders whether it isn't María Angélica who's now affecting a strategic retreat. If such is the case, he's best off keeping his mouth shut. Exaggeratedly, painstakingly, then, he studies his well-ordered record library, seizing on this moment to give his new record its proper place beside Corelli's sonatas. Next he wanders into the kitchen, opens the refrigerator, and, glancing inside, notices a bottle of Suter where the Cokes usually stand. Shutting the refrigerator door, he returns to the living room, all the while reflecting on his situation.

First off, he wants to analyze the information that, de-

74

spite the countless turns of their conversation, his oracle has passed on to him. What was that information? First answer: She'd save him. Yes, sir, she'd save him (and her words were accompanied by an affirmative movement of her head). Second answer: She wouldn't get mixed up in it, really (this time a negative movement of her head).

Which is to say that, as usual, María Angélica had cast all superfluous details aside and reduced the matter to its essence. And there the problem stood, clear and simple. In one case yes, she said; in the other no. Straight as an arrow.

All right, but no matter how simple, clear, intelligent, or honest her setting out the question may have been, it still isn't a solution. And what Sanctis was expecting from María Angélica—anxiously, childishly—was a solution. He wanted to know what to do at this particular juncture and not in the hypothetical cases they had talked about in their hit-or-miss way.

Like a pitiless light illuminating everything degree by degree, Sanctis feels a horrendous certainty rising in him—the certainty that María Angélica can't do anything for him, can't help him, can't provide the magic solution that with almost religious faith he'd been expecting from her. It seems stupid, but only now, after he has spoken to his wife for some thirty or so minutes, is this simple, terrifying truth fully driven home to him. It's no longer a matter of the right cloth for a suit or the right school to send the kids to or what ideas he should put forward at a meeting of the owners of the apartment house. This time he's dealing with a matter that's dangerous and that really can't be talked about, a matter he has obviously to settle by himself and as best he can.

And this clear view, this awareness that María Angélica can't help him, fills him with foreboding. Once more he goes back to feeling alone in a vast city, alone in the world, and completely helpless. That can't be María Angélica there reading by the lamp, her glasses slipped down on her nose, playing with a button of her blouse. The real María Angélica, his wife-mother, his bestower of peace and understanding, must at this moment be far, far away, thousands of miles from this living room. And the person sitting there in her place now is someone strange, someone unknown to him, someone with whom communication is impossible.

Paradoxically, this feeling of loneliness makes him need to be alone again. He wants to think in peace about this mess which, thanks to Elena Vaccaro's foolishness or irresponsibility, he's stuck in. He's got to make up his mind what he will do and won't do in the coming hours. He admits to himself he's scared.

He knows he must get out of the house at once and walk. Also smoke a cigarette without having to explain anything to his wife. He approaches María Angélica, saying, "I'm going out for a walk. I'm not sleepy."

María Angélica keeps a finger on the line she was reading, lifts her head, and asks if he'll be long. The question is accompanied (something he wasn't at all expecting) by a certain tone and a sleepy smile that Sanctis knows well and that have to do with bed, with a certain French perfume that only now he's aware he's been smelling without being conscious of it, and of course with the bottle of Suter he spied in the refrigerator. (Sanctis reflects that Zen Buddhism can't be as boring as María Angélica makes out, that it obviously possesses, at the very least, some unexpected qualities.)

"Uh . . . no. I'm just going to stretch my legs a bit and I'll be right back."

"If Perugia calls again, what shall I tell him?" asks María Angélica.

"It's all right. Maybe I'll take a swing by his place. So please don't stay up waiting for me. In any case, I won't be very long."

He kisses María Angélica and leaves.

CHAPTER IX

In which Francisco Sanctis finds it necessary to order the other Francisco Sanctis to quit the scene, and an incipient erection—even if somewhat ill-timed—comes in one fell swoop to solve the whole knot of problems

Not until he reaches the corner of Cramer, a distance of two cautious blocks from his apartment, does Sanctis dare light up a cigarette. Badly needing it, he sucks the smoke in deep. At the same time, he wiggles his shoulders comically, as if trying to make himself relax, and presses the side of his mouth with his thumb. This last seems to mean, Let's cut out the crap and use our head like a responsible adult male.

Once and for all—it simply can't be avoided any longer—he must come to grips with this messy state of affairs which for some reason or other he's foolishly taken on himself but which on second thought he may come to see is really none of his business.

To make matters worse, it dawns on him that by having relied too heavily on María Angélica's supposed infallibility he's let time slip by, and the solution, which is absolutely necessary, is no nearer.

Looking on himself as a sensible, intelligent man, he sees he must deal with the problem in the most objective possible way—in other words, distance himself from the facts and not let Elena Vaccaro's insidious pressurizing or her more or less subliminal messages (couched in sly flattery and hypnotic red sweaters) interfere with his ability to reason. Nor, for that matter, must he let his shaky state of mind affect him. (He readily admits that for a while now he's been a bit edgy, a mass of unfounded fears.) The thing to do—he's almost speechifying—is to analyze everything coolly and from the very beginning. Okay, then.

He spoke these last words aloud, exhaling through his nose and allowing for a proper rhetorical pause. Then, figuratively speaking, he sits back comfortably to contemplate the ever-instructive spectacle of his brain ticking over in a sound, well-balanced manner. He's in the midst of setting out the premises of some irrefutable syllogism, when *whoom!* something intrudes on the scene like a stray dog wandering in off the street. This distracts him. It has an element of the perverse about it, akin to whistling the same catchy, trashy music over and over again, and he finds himself like an utter boob repeating the scribbled addresses on the slip of paper, which, of course, he still remembers to the letter.

"Álvarez Thomas 2837, Lacarra 4225," he says.

And that's not all. There seems to be another Francisco Sanctis—obsessed, programmed like a robot, and completely oblivious—going his own way unperturbed, only to find himself uttering these puzzling words:

"What time is it? Eleven. They usually come in the early hours, she said. So—"

Luckily, he recovers at once. Pulling out the plug on the robot, he forces the side of Francisco Sanctis that's a bit loony back onto the straight and narrow, rebukes himself, and asks what in hell's name he's mouthing and what all this ridiculous concern with the clock is about. Clearing his throat, he returns to his conscientious sifting of the facts.

Once the intrusive dog has been ushered out and the crazy Francisco Sanctis conveniently silenced by the real Francisco Sanctis, the latter, as a step in the direction of sanity, tries to separate the hard facts from purely subjective considerations (the out-and-out crap, to put a name to it), which must have been stealthily filtering into his mind, serving only to confuse issues still further. But all's not as simple as it seems. Why not? Well, in the first place, because the dividing line between certainty and doubt isn't all that clear-cut. Why on earth, for example, must he accept as hard facts the secret information revealed to him from the lips of a woman—a woman in smart casual clothes—about whom he knows only the handful of things she felt like telling him? And all this inside a Renault that kept turning and turning like a merry-go-round.

And in the second place, even if for a moment or two, faced with such basic evidence as a certain sad little smile or an ambiguous shake of the head, Sanctis began to convince himself that this time Elena wasn't lying, it has to be admitted—speaking seriously now—that there's no reason whatever to think that Elena, today in November 1977, is no longer the same spinner of yarns she was in the old days, when the most dogged of the CIA's sleuths never lost her scent for a single second. It has also to be admitted that it was his own ingenuousness or foolishness, together with that hothouse atmosphere of erotic persecution there in the car, that caused Sanctis to be led by the nose and with the greatest of ease straight into Elena Vaccaro's crazy world (aided, of course, by his own fruitcake imagination), where he ended up buying—cash down and no haggling—all the crap Elena wanted to unload on him. And so the much-touted Julio Cardini and Bernardo Lipstein don't even exist. Or if they do, if they are not mere figments of Elenita Vaccaro's feverish imagination, they won't be sitting around their respective homes on Álvarez Thomas and Lacarra streets, waiting like fools to be turned into pap for various intelligence agencies. Is it not logical to suppose that they've sneaked off somewhere or other, or, what's even more probable, are comfortably out of harm's way in Mexico or Spain?

In other words, to start out by calling Elenita Vaccaro's patchwork information hard facts and to wind up in a James Bond film as a result (as well as for other weighty reasons, such as having published one little poem almost twenty years before), or to justify the halo of fighter and rebel that funnily enough has been set around his incipient baldness, would be to fall into the same daydreaming, middle-class, romantic dizziness as this new Elenita—the sportswoman, weight watcher, traveler, hairdresser and beauty salon front-liner, probable fraud, and definite loony.

Which is to say nothing doing. Sanctis is crossing Amenábar, heading toward Cabildo, when, exhaling again, he turns down his mouth as if he were saying, "Who's fooling who?" Then, shaking his head, he actually says, "Nothing doing."

Nothing at all, because, as usual, Elenita is completely off the mark. And also because if in the whole of this lousy city there's one guy not in the least suited for the thing they're trying to foist on him now, surely that guy is him. No two ways about it. Here he is, someone who's been out of any sort of political activity for a thousand years; who has his own opinions, naturally, but who for some time now has made his peace with the world; someone with a modest job and an apartment on Monroe Street; someone married to and in love with a woman like María Angélica, the father of three wonderful kids, who buries himself every chance he gets in his beloved Handel and Boccherini. What in shit's name has he to do with this mad comic strip about a couple of guys being hunted down by an intelligence agency; about husbands who aren't involved in it, or pretend they aren't involved; about information which—this can't be brushed aside—may well be a trap; about black Ford Falcons that cruise the city like phantoms; about murderers armed with Ithakas and submachine guns;

about torturers who at three in the morning climb into their cars, slipping the safety catches off their weapons; about lousy sons of bitches heading for Álvarez Thomas 2837 and Lacarra—

At this point, the other Francisco Sanctis bursts into the sentence unannounced, twisting its meaning and distorting the eloquent exposition with belligerent, unhelpful imagery. This forces the real Francisco Sanctis to give him another good tongue-lashing and to cast him straight into a dark cellar from which he mustn't be let out, from which there's no reason he should show his crazy head ever again—especially now, when the real Sanctis is trying to shed a bit of light on this whole untidy mess. Christ!

This over (and the last drag on his cigarette accompanied by an angry gesture meaning "Christ!"), Sanctis returns to his solitary speech and, free of interference, declares sagely that there are probably those with special skills who could profit, as is only right, from the information so stupidly and hastily dumped on him. Members of some organization, for example, who, in the shrewd words of the Mata Hari of the elegant Barrio Norte, "know what to do in these cases." Guys who, furthermore, have themselves chosen their ironclad path, a path very different from the one chosen by him—another aspect of the question that has to be taken into account. Here he pauses to mull over his own words and then continues: Because nobody can deny that in his day he, too, made his contribution. Hadn't he been a political activist for almost two years? Hadn't he had to endure the chases, the tear gas, the nights without sleep, and even the occasional blows to his ribs from a cop's truncheon? Can it be said that Francisco Sanctis is a coward? No, sir, it cannot. And if not, let them ask any of his comrades of that era—or for that matter, Elena herself. Yes, Elenita Vaccaro, *Fist on High*'s business manager, who for some reason or other, among twenty or thirty candidates, has singled out him for this impossible mission.

Ah, highly honored by the distinction, but it turns out that he can't accept it because—well, because just now he finds himself involved in another kind of struggle. What kind of struggle? Well, sir, he says as if to launch into a polemic, not with the other Francisco Sanctis, shut away in the cellar and for the moment not wanting to show his nose, but with a speaker unknown yet a lot more reasonable and intelligent than that scatterbrain. Well, sir, I'll explain straightaway. The struggle for spiritual values. You understand perfectly what I'm talking about, don't you? True freedom—that's it—true freedom in a world rotten with corruption and utilitarian values. That's not much, you think. I'm talking about the struggle to rescue at least one individual, one alone, out of this miasma of stupidity and violence in which we're plunged up to our necks.

So then, he continues, thoroughly wrapped up in the controversy, to abandon the struggle, to turn away cowardly from the struggle (yes, sir, that's what I said—cowardly) for something that in the end is only accidental, a siren song, let us say, would be to sell myself out, to sell out my own chosen way, my own ideals. Crazy, isn't it?

And all this—in aid of what? In aid of something that, yes, of course, can also be a respectable ideal; I don't mind admitting it. Not at all. But speaking with absolute honesty, an ideal I don't understand that well and maybe don't altogether share. Why not come out and say so?

At this point he interrupts his vehement address to Mr. X to go back and tell himself in the same categorical tone of a short while ago, "Nothing doing. Definitely not."

And with both head and hands he makes a gesture as if to scare off a bothersome horsefly.

Meanwhile, he's reached Cabildo, has looked with a pang of misgiving at a man talking into the interior of a parked car, has turned left on Cabildo, and is now about to cross Quesada. Without set purpose, he's heading in the direction of Puente Saavedra.

Crossing Quesada, completely absorbed in his thoughts, he fails to notice a car moving slowly toward the avenue, and he nearly walks straight into it. He only makes it out when it's less than a foot from his nose. It's a patrol car, with four men inside. It gives him the fright of his life, but he does his best to put on a vacuous expression, executes a sort of bullfight pass or a tango step, and slips behind the car to gain the curb.

The fear comes flooding back. He's sure the four cops (two uniformed, two in civilian clothes) were looking at him a mite too closely. Suddenly he's made uneasy by the nagging impression that those names and addresses he thought were carefully hidden in his memory have somehow become objects—flashing, clinking, betraying—that any cop could easily spot just by looking Sanctis up and down.

His childish gesture of raising a hand to his forehead as if to cover something hidden within makes him laugh, stops him short, and he tries to take himself a bit less seriously. He tells himself that despite the much-vaunted computerized fingerprinting device said to be carried in patrol cars, and any number of other sophisticated gadgets used, it is rumored, by the various security agencies, a device to read people's minds still hasn't been invented. If such a gadget existed, either on political grounds or on grounds of public decency there'd be nobody free to walk the streets.

But in fact this little joke doesn't altogether allay his fears. He still feels naked, transparent, vulnerable, exposed from one moment to the next to the possibility of an unpleasant encounter with the cops, and if that happened he honestly wouldn't know how the hell to behave.

He comes to the healthy conclusion that walking alone in the street at that hour isn't going to do him any good. Rather the reverse: this wandering about that he thought necessary for sorting out his ideas has only increased the formless fears that he began feeling a while ago and that here, in the dead of night along deserted, police-ridden Cabildo, are becoming almost intolerable.

He tells himself that the best thing, then, is to finish this pointless stroll at once, turn right around, and go straight home. On the spot, he has a mad urge to get back to his apartment, relax in a good long shower, and go to bed. María Angélica would still be awake, probably having just turned in.

Like a fool, he stands there thinking about María Angélica, about María Angélica's warm skin, about María Angélica's waist and thighs, about María Angélica's taste and smell, about how María Angélica is his oasis, his haven, his rock, his warm lap. He also thinks about her smile when she asked if he'd be long, about the French perfume and the nice bottle of Suter waiting in the refrigerator, and suddenly he discovers he has a semi-erection.

Despite his years of marriage, making love to María Angélica still has about it something magical and unpredictable. He also knows he has only to let himself sink into that swell of tender dizziness, playful obscenities, devotion, and frenzy for all the world's problems to recede as if by magic.

He admits to himself that the only thing he really wants at this moment is to be back with María Angélica, and even if out of pure inertia he's still heading for Puente Saavedra, he gives a determined nod of his head to tell himself that that's exactly what he'll do.

It astonishes him that everything's been resolved so easily, that just thinking about María Angélica was enough for the solution to appear in a flash. He decides to walk on a few more blocks to clear his mind, checks the time, and promises himself he'll be back home before midnight.

The two names and addresses have turned into superfluous objects, then, absurd trifles that he doesn't have to hang on to now, since they no longer serve a purpose. By a rather less rational method than the one he had intended at the outset of his walk, he has at last made up his mind. What's the point, then, of keeping that series of words and numbers in his head? He must simply cast all that into oblivion right now, get out from under, toss it aside like the useless, troublesome burden it is.

But this time he doesn't feel like justifying the decision he's just made to anyone—not even his understanding interlocutor. The erection's still with him, and this disposes him, instead, to put his faith in a summons, a sort of telepathic communication he has received from María Angélica, which he has perfectly understood and which is worth—of this he has no doubt—all the reasoning in the world.

Now all becomes transparently clear. Elena Vaccaro's little fantasy has as much to do with him as the rebellion of the Kurds or the electrification of Villa Soldati. In a word, it's none of his business. And as he won't be seeing Elena again, nor will the occasion to talk about this with anyone arise, the best thing would be to lay the whole business to rest then and there.

Because the funny thing about all this is . . .

CHAPTER X

*In which nothing seems to have changed except
that the telepathic erection has disappeared, and with it
the possibility of performing acts both beautiful and unexpected, and Sanctis, who continues his walk along
Cabildo, comes upon a couple of young layabouts on
Paroissien Street*

. . . the funny thing about all this is that Elena never
even gave him a chance to excuse himself or just plain
refuse. Excuse himself from what? Refuse what? This is
what Sanctis is thinking—despite what he had decided
with such spiritual and physiological firmness only a
few seconds ago—as he continues walking toward
Puente Saavedra. If Elena proposed nothing, neither did
she explicitly ask for anything. The only thing she did,
when you come right down to it, was to rid herself with
relative elegance of a small problem and palm it off on
him. But no, he corrects himself, not even a small problem, just a scrap of information—a dubious scrap of information obtained he can't imagine how—that she
quickly passed on to him the way someone passes on a
tip about a sure thing in the sixth at Palermo on Sunday,

or better, the way one drops a handle that's burning one's fingers. Simple as that.

A rather comfortable way—if judged rightfully—of putting a pretty muzzle on her conscience, the conscience of a guilt-ridden little bourgeoise and wife of a brass hat to boot (in other words, a witness to and possibly an accomplice in who the hell knows what amount of shit), and staying at peace with herself. Wonderful, isn't it? Because more than likely the bitch must feel deliciously at peace just now. Maybe she even considers herself some kind of Molly Pitcher, and tomorrow no doubt she'll be explaining the whole thing to a friend or her lover of the moment or her analyst. What with her independent means, her reading of Simone de Beauvoir, her enrollment in parapsychology and body expression courses, and being an adulteress on moral principle, there'll be plenty to talk about, you can be sure of that. Meanwhile, indirectly, she'll be appeasing that tireless roly-poly girl with the reform-school shoes who from back there in distant adolescence must stare at her now and again with accusing (and bespectacled) eyes.

Well, he's beginning to see things clearly, thank God, and he's not going to put himself at Elenita Vaccaro's disposal to assuage her rotten guilt. That'd be the limit.

He's now come as far as Republiquetas, and he reckons that if he wants to get back before María Angélica goes to sleep he should catch a bus right there. Approaching the stop, he leans against the signpost and waits. The night is pleasantly cool. A niggling breeze has sprung up, stirring the leaves on the trees and dragging disorderly litter along the street. The problems of the day are beginning to take effect, and Sanctis is all in. Drowsily, he stands there gawking at the pavement, the eddies of dust at the street corners, the sky that begins to cloud over and that may be threatening rain. His eyes sting; he's sleepy.

He doesn't know what on earth could have been going through his head, because at some point his attention wandered and he let an almost empty 68 bus go by. It'll be fifteen minutes at least before another will be along. Bad luck.

He's bored being stuck there, and he'd rather walk for a few blocks. To the next stop, he tells himself. He moves on again in the direction of Puente Saavedra.

Making his way reluctantly, almost dragging his feet, he leaves García del Río behind him and then Manzanares. At a distance of twenty-five or so yards from the corner of Paroissien Street, he sees two young men standing at the bus stop. At once, and without knowing exactly why, he decides to continue on his way.

Hands in his pockets and trying to look bored, a nonentity, he observes them out of the corner of his eye. They are boys. One's in sneakers and jeans and wears a dark jacket that's miles too big for him. Tall, very thin, and carrying a blue bag in his hand, he has to stoop a bit to talk to his friend. The friend, stocky and with a mop of curly fair hair, has a Jewish look about him. As Sanctis draws alongside, they break off their conversation and, with an air of indifference (too much indifference), look toward the far end of Cabildo as if trying to spot the next bus. Activists, Sanctis diagnoses.

He doesn't even turn his head for a good look at their faces, but just then the spark of an idea begins playing around in his head. What if he approached these two right now and, straight out, without any fancy preliminaries, passed the names and addresses on to them? What if he went and told them, Look, boys, want to make a note of this, please? Julio Cardini, Álvarez Thomas 2837, third floor, apartment C; Bernardo Lipstein, Lacarra 4225. Okay, I want you to know they're going to be nabbed tonight. You heard me. No questions, please; that's all I can say. You two know what you have to do. Good night.

Because obviously these two must belong to some organization. In other words, they know what's going on and they know what to do in a case like this. Great, perfect, fine. Just pass on the information and bye-bye. If I've seen you somewhere before, I can't remember where or when. And in this way Sanctis gets rid of his little burden, at the same time doing something useful, something decent. All in all, it's not a bad idea.

He slows his step. He comes to a stop and is about to turn back. But no sooner has his body started to respond than he quickly changes his mind and strides off, trying to get the corner of Paroissien Street behind him as soon as possible.

He accuses himself of being foolish and naive. He tells himself that his thoughts are becoming as delirious as Elenita Vaccaro's. That the barbarism he'd nearly committed would only have occurred to an utter madman. Because, let's face it, where the hell did he get it from that these two guys were political activists? Didn't the cops nowadays often dress up like students or salesmen or even hippies? And what if at best this pair weren't cops but pure louts and informers, and they'd turned him in? God, it's obvious that weariness is making him rave.

Anyway, hasn't he just made up his mind once and for all? If so, why is he fishing around for a candidate to pass the bundle on to? What is this, a relay race? A chain letter? Make two copies of this letter and send them immediately to two persons of your acquaintance. Balbino Gutiérrez, from Buenos Aires, didn't, and a wardrobe fell on his head. Cesáreo Giambattista, from Rosario, did, and an aunt in Catanzaro left him an inheritance. What is this, a clever dodge for him, too, to be rid of a small burden of conscience? To cover his bets? So the wardrobe won't come down on his head? No, no, dear friend, just a moment. He has no reason either to gag or to ease his conscience. Has he ever collaborated with the military regime? Has he in any way supported it? No, sir, just the opposite. At heart, he's always held them in contempt for having brought the country to ruin. For being murderers, sure, but more than anything for being bullies and brutes.

And now it comes back to him how as a result of his stifled hatred of the regime and a certain secret admiration for those who were out risking life and limb fighting against the armed forces, Sanctis once made hesitant overtures to some of these unknown young men via Lu-cho. Sanctis's intentions were never very clear, to tell the truth, but he did give it a try. He remembers that the thing didn't come off, and that Lucho's attitude, which was mistrustful and evasive, left him at a loss, suspected maybe of being a useless busybody or a stool pigeon. Still, this unimportant fact, he tells himself, shows up his stance in an unmistakable way. Not just his present stance toward the military dictatorship, but his whole life. And his fearlessness too—Christ!—during that whole time at least.

On the other hand, the attempt was neither as absurd nor as pointless as it seemed, and that was being proved now. Give him one guy, just one reliable guy among the bunch, and he'd be home free.

No, the sudden idea of handing over his information to someone with more experience and better connected than he wasn't all that absurd. What was absurd, he now admits, was to come to the conclusion in such an arbitrary way that the two young guys there on Paroissien Street were activists. But that's a horse of another color.

Because if he knew someone, any boy at all, more or less linked to one of these groups with the mysterious acronyms, the thing would be relatively easy. He'd search for him, he'd pass on the information, and in no time at all the salvage operation would be on its way. Or if he knew some guy who knew someone who knew someone . . .

But no, it just fucking happens that Francisco Sanctis, the bookkeeper, doesn't know and hasn't the slightest connection with a single subversive (to use the bad word). Which is to say, he knows the Fernández kid, but has anyone any idea of Lucho's whereabouts right now? Besides, Sanctis doesn't want to be a pessimist, but is it likely that Lucho is still alive? Does anyone know? One hears about so many atrocities: concentration camps, mangled corpses dumped here and there, bodies dynamited or seen floating in the River Plate. It doesn't bear thinking about.

And there are also Lucho's parents, of course, the Fernándezes—above all Rita, the mother, a friend of María Angélica's. But after the raid on their house and the start of the despicable phone threats, the Fernándezes left their bungalow on Blanco Encalada Street, and, of course, they kept their new address secret. So that leaves the Fernándezes out.

In other words, of a contact, of whatever's meant by a contact, sweet fuck all. And to think that Elena's phone call as well as the subsequent delivery of the bundle came about only because it was assumed that he, Francisco Sanctis, maintained close ties with the upper crust of subversive elements. Couldn't you split your sides laughing? Shouldn't all this be taken as a joke, something he can one day tell as the funniest joke of 1977?

But no, it's nothing to split your sides about. Rather, it's food for thought, Sanctis tells himself as, crossing Besares Street, he philosophically kicks a pebble. Because if in spite of admiring these young people, in spite of his confused desire to approach them, he doesn't know a single person who can give him a hand now, or even anyone he can rely on or ask advice of, it means that the years, or his job, or his marriage, or Christ knows what else, have set him apart from what once played an important role in his life.

Yes, this seems to be so, he admits, and no doubt it's a subject to go into some other time, yet by the same token it's an equally good reason not to be splitting hairs now but to go ahead and tell oneself that the thing just isn't going to work out. Because now it all looks perfectly logical. Elena's words were quite clear. "It would be a lot better if it weren't you. Better someone who didn't know you, let alone me." Plain as the nose on your face. He mustn't do it. It needs some guy who doesn't know him. All right. He doesn't know anyone who fits that bill. So the thing becomes rather impossible. In other words, Elena has presented him at one and the same time with the problem and the solution. Meaning that the problem solves itself. How does it solve itself? Very simply. By his doing absolutely nothing. By just staying put.

Unaware, he has passed one or even two bus stops. He's only a few blocks from the city limits, and he decides to make his way to the terminal, where he can catch any of several buses. Quarter to twelve. María Angélica must be asleep by now. No sense breaking his neck, then, and he drops back to his slow pace. There's a steady blow now. The night has almost turned cold— nice for walking. Tomorrow's Saturday, he thinks, he doesn't have to go to the office, and this stroll, which is gradually calming his nerves, has been worth it.

He takes out a cigarette. To light a match he has to lean into a doorway, sheltering behind his lapel. He manages it in the end, lifts his head, and takes a first deep drag. Just then he looks toward the next street corner. He sees two people hurriedly turning away from Cabildo and heading down Ramallo. He can barely make them out, but he thinks they might be the two boys from Paroissien Street. Strange, isn't it? All right, maybe they weren't really waiting for a bus. Maybe they got ahead of him just now by walking on the opposite side of the street.

He wants to have a look at them from close up. Silly, but since he was thinking about them so much, he wants to see if . . .

He starts to lean forward in the direction of Ramallo, about to break into a trot. He holds back. What's the point of looking at them close up? To find out if they really are the same two? To verify his intuition that they're political activists? It's more than silly. It's screwy. If they're members of some group, they're going to take him for a cop. If not, they'll take him for a queer. Besides, why all this interest in two guys he barely caught a glimpse of in passing?

As if playing at some game, he tries to remember them. One was dark-haired and skinny; the other stocky, with curly blond hair. At that very moment, *ting-a-ling, ting-a-ling,* the metaphorical and all but audible alarm bell goes off, and once more the names Julio Cardini and Bernardo Lipstein are revolving restlessly in the recesses of his mind, the tiny lights pulsing clearly on the panel.

This time he is unaffected. He simply decides to ignore this new breakout into the domain of common sense by the crazy, stashed-away Francisco Sanctis. The real Sanctis turns up his lapels, whistles faintly, and continues his walk along Cabildo.

Only after a block or more does he begin to put the two together—the boys on Paroissien Street and the names that for a while there were like small signs flashing in the dark. All at once, leaping out from some corner of his mind with the brilliance of an exploding firework, comes an idea—a notion, rather—that brings him up short. What if they were them? he wonders.

It seems fantastic, of course, but after all it isn't impossible. And his head, really worn out by this time of night, begins toying with the idea. What if those two guys, the pair who just disappeared down Ramallo, were none other than Julio Cardini and Bernardo Lipstein? And what if chance or fate or God or Christ knows who tossed them under his nose just like that, perhaps to test him or offer him an opportunity?

And what if he were to turn around right now and start running toward Ramallo and caught up with them? How neat, how perfect it would be. He'd signal to them with a hand and call them by name. Naturally they'd stop, scared a bit at first maybe, but as soon as he spoke to them they'd calm down. Then, right there, the message. A few well-chosen, decisive words and that's it. He'd turn around and disappear. And in this way, simply, methodically, expertly, he'd save those two boys' lives, he'd prevent them from being hunted down later that night by those Air Force sons of bitches. Not bad, eh?

Sure, of course, a fantasy, a lovely fairy tale which now, barely two blocks from Ramallo, he no longer believes in, finding it a product of his weariness. For reasons of sanity, he wants to get it out of his head.

But he can't. The fantasy, the notion, keeps buzzing round him like a horsefly. And what's worse, it has the extraordinary power to open the floodgates to new ideas, to new images that hadn't revealed themselves before now with such horrible clarity. He's left with a bitter taste in his mouth, a feeling akin to anguish.

What new ideas? Well, nothing unusual. Simply these: Sanctis, despite himself, keeps thinking about those two young men on Paroissien Street, who may be the same two as on Ramallo Street. He tells himself that if this pair could have been (for one moment, and only in his imagination, of course) Julio Cardini and Bernardo Lipstein, it means quite simply that Julio Cardini and Bernardo Lipstein exist. There is, after all, a difference between living persons and ghosts or abstractions. Undeniably, this may be a platitude or a piece of nonsense, but it's still true that until now Sanctis hadn't altogether accepted, hadn't dared accept, such a simple, obvious fact. It hadn't entered his mind—he hadn't wanted it to enter his mind until now—that Julio Cardini and Bernardo Lipstein, like the two boys, have faces, hair of a certain color, shoes, a particular smell, some aunt maybe, a football team of which they are fans, a certain way of pronouncing their *s*'s, and whatnot. No more to it than that—an obvious, silly truism. But suddenly, and by an absurd somersault of his imagination, Julio Cardini and Bernardo Lipstein have stopped being two names scribbled on the back of an optician's receipt and then learned by heart, and are real people—men, unknown men, sure, but alive and with a body like his and with inconsistent, restless minds like his. And maybe with the same fear he's feeling at this moment, a fear that little by little is oppressing him, paralyzing him.

CHAPTER XI

In which Sanctis shrewdly decides to throw in all but one of his cards, as a result of which fate takes up the pack and quickly deals him more, one of which, glanced at rather riskily from the middle of Maipú Avenue, may not be too bad after all

Stepping up onto the Vedia Street sidewalk, Sanctis misses his footing, stumbles, and nearly falls flat on his face. Only now does it dawn on him that for the past few minutes his legs have been a bit shaky.

He's familiar with the feeling. He tells himself he's scared, scared shitless, and why not call a spade a spade? From out of the past, from the fringes of adolescence after he quit the seminary, from the weeds and tin cans of some vacant lot, he feels the horrible jelliness in the legs that used to come over him like the onset of an illness seconds before he got mixed up in a fistfight.

It always started with a coldness in the pit of his stomach, as if he were about to be sick; then came a stiffening of the jaw which literally prevented him from uttering a word; and, hard on that, the wobbliness that invaded his legs. Somehow he felt his feet weren't in contact with the ground; he felt suspended in midair, as weightless as a sheet of paper, and in danger of toppling over at the slightest push. Exactly what he's feeling now, but without any seeming justification for it.

All this strikes him as senseless, even a tiny bit funny. A fight was a fight, implying a certain risk. So that the fear that preceded it—primal and animal-like—was understandable. But right now, during this innocent stroll along Cabildo to Puente Saavedra, what has precipitated this fear? What step is he about to take, what risk, that can explain this caving in of his legs?

None, absolutely none. Luckily, this is crystal clear to him. Hasn't he once and for all put the lid on the Elena Vaccaro affair? Where on earth, then, is this irrational fear coming from?

Some sort of physiological mechanism brings back to him the coldness in the stomach, the paralyzed jaw, the wobbly legs—the fear, in a word—which vanished in the heat of the first punches. Fear turned to blind courage in a flurry of blows that, in spite of his nonexistent boxing style, allowed him to pass that brutal test of manhood.

All right, he just about got through those tests, and even today, thirty years on, he still derives some childish comfort from it. But right now, at his time of life, what the hell is this test he's facing?

This feeling of being put to a test seems so crazy, so weird, that he tries to make light of it by dreaming up a new and highly unlikely meeting with the red sweater in the shadowy interior of the Renault, this time minus the burned bits of paper and the spouses.

But the idea doesn't really get off the ground. As if two pairs of eyes (one dark with long lashes, the other gray or green, lurking behind a lock of tight curls) were staring at him, Sanctis suddenly loses interest in all this nonsense. He brushes his fingertips along a wall, looks down at his feet, and willy-nilly his thoughts return to Julio Cardini and Bernardo Lipstein.

Julio Cardini and Bernardo Lipstein, whose names no longer appear to Sanctis written on an optician's receipt but, as of tonight, on an Air Force Intelligence mimeographed list, with a significant tiny check mark penciled beside them. Julio Cardini and Bernardo Lipstein, unaware of course of this tiny mark, may be fast asleep, or drinking maté, or fornicating, or writing something down on a notepad, or feeding the canary, or painting the kitchen table, unconcerned perhaps, or worried sick, or scared to death like nearly everyone else these days; Julio Cardini and Bernardo Lipstein, hurrying along like the two young men on Ramallo Street, or riding a bus, or sitting in a café, or there in their own homes at Álvarez Thomas 2837 and Lacarra 4225—whatever they're doing, oblivious of the decision made that afternoon by some two-bit Air Force captain or colonel over a cup of coffee in an office at HQ. In other words, Cardini and Lipstein living out their everyday lives, living their wonderful, chaotic lives, not knowing . . .

Not knowing what? Let's see. Sanctis asks himself the question in a tone of weary impatience, of exhaustion, of undisguised tedium. Maybe he's trying to provoke or defy the questioner, the unbidden, naive Francisco Sanc-

103

tis, whom he must stop in his tracks, realizing, luckily this time, that the innocent little question will come laden with malice and turn into yet another stinking trap. If he lets his imagination go down that slippery path, all the peace of mind achieved by decisive thinking and by his detailed plans for going to bed shortly with María Angélica—who's ripe for the picking, thanks to Zen Buddhism, French perfume, and the bottle waiting in the refrigerator—all his precious, longed-for peace of mind will come to grief, driven there by the inevitable consequence of answering the tricky little question. This is why the sentence must remain unfinished, stopping at the words "not knowing," and then losing its way and moving on to something else. All of which is completely reasonable, since there's no need for anyone to speculate to anyone else about what two guys called Julio Cardini and Bernardo Lipstein know or don't know tonight. What's the point of playing around with blind assumptions?

So it's best to leave well enough alone and change the subject at once, since it's no longer possible to patch up the sentence by saying, for instance, "not knowing they're coming for them tonight," because "they're coming for them tonight" has been—and was until a few seconds ago—a creepy but a simple sentence after all, just a way of saying that somewhere or other tonight at the appointed hour, Air Force Intelligence will carry out their nauseating procedure of picking guys up and beating them to a pulp. But no, it's already late even for a patch-up job, because in the same way that Julio Cardini and Bernardo Lipstein at some moment stopped being merely names scribbled on a slip of paper and became outrageously alive, the words "they're coming for them tonight" strive and strain in some part of his loony imagination to become more than that simple sentence. A shoot beginning to sprout, pushing up the earth, now its first leaves unfolding, now its branches reaching up unhindered, and then "they're coming for them tonight" is no longer that dry string of words. Some propitiously fertilized soil feeds it, filling it with an unknown sap; it grows monstrously, suddenly turning into a bungalow with a privet hedge and unplastered walls in a tree-lined street in Villa Lugano; it turns into a third-floor apartment in a building with gray balconies in Villa Urquiza, outside which several Ford Falcons are silently parked; it turns into those shiny black cars whose doors swing open without a sound and into men getting out, all of them in civilian clothes, some wearing denim jackets and jeans, and the oiled barrel of an Ithaka glinting under the light of a street lamp or the moon; it turns into a front walk and the stairs these men are climbing, and into the din of doors being kicked in. "They're coming for them tonight," and Julio Cardini and Bernardo Lipstein, together now, thrown on the concrete floor of some Air Force building, hoods over their heads, every inch of their bodies broken by torture, bleeding from the mouth and genitals. "They're coming for them tonight," and two guys, one tall and thin, the other brawny with curly hair, Julio Cardini and Bernardo Lipstein, dumped on the floor of an airplane and together with others hurled out of the plane's cargo door, their swollen bodies against the brown waters of the river, perhaps washed up by the current on some Uruguayan beach, to the horror and revulsion of . . .

Sanctis's face grows tense in a grimace of disgust. He feels sick. He curses his imagination, which is determined to force on him this horrendous nightmare. No, shit no, this can't possibly be what they placed in his hands. This can't be what Elena Vaccaro's stupidity or diabolical cunning has placed in his hands like a small gift. Something's wrong here. Nobody with an iota of common sense can believe that everything depends on him, on what he does or doesn't do tonight. Come on. This is obviously a misunderstanding, another clever sidetrack on the part of his imagination, but this time he's not falling for it—no, sir. Because among other reasons, there isn't the faintest possibility of his doing anything, since in the completely unlikely event that he wanted to do something, Elena Vaccaro's own words would soon clear his head of any such notion. Hadn't she said quite plainly that it would be better if he found someone else? Fine. And then what? Who the hell ever imagined this was his thing?

He spreads his arms in a gesture straight out of an Italian movie, making it clear that the problem is none of his business. Sighing, he tries to calm down again. Impossible. His mind won't stop churning away. He looks for something to busy himself with, and out of sheer perversity he goes over again all he remembers of his conversation with Elena Vaccaro, perhaps in search of new or forgotten grounds for his decision.

It's a mistake. Yes, but by the time he sees this it's too late. Because it's obvious that tonight words, all words, have a life of their own. And now suddenly he discovers that the phrase "it would be better" means just that, that it would be better. In other words, it's not an outright prohibition, an impossibility, but means something else. Supposing, for example, he doesn't get in touch with the famous contacts (those mysterious persons who know what to do, and so forth). All right, only in that instance, though it isn't exactly the best solution, no one has expressly forbidden Sanctis from somehow or other doing whatever he can do. Of course, he still doesn't know exactly what he can do short of landing up to his neck in trouble or falling like a fool into a hypothetical trap set by some Air Force genius for Elena Vaccaro or her little hubby. But by now it's all too much for his weary head.

An "Oh, my God!" of sheer desperation escapes from his lips. He lights another cigarette. He executes a sort of karate chop with the edge of his hand. He gazes up at the sky as if some help might be forthcoming from that quarter. How come this whole affair is still buzzing around his head like a horsefly? How come he still hasn't been able to swat this fly dead?

Without noticing, he's made his way past the thick concrete columns and under the bridge crossed by General Paz Avenue. He's facing Maipú Avenue, only a few steps from the bus terminal. Casting a glance along the sidewalk, he spots an open bar.

Up till now there must have been a faulty contact in his brain. Just then, like a dictate from the gods, he's struck by what has to be his best idea that night. What idea's that? To give María Angélica a little ring right now and tell her he'll be home in five minutes.

It could be a stupid thing to do. It's nearly midnight, and María Angélica must be fast asleep. Waking her up to listen to his nonsense will give her about as much pleasure as someone trampling on her corn. Never mind. It's a calculated risk. But it's absolutely necessary if he wants everything to work out as planned. Why? Because phoning María Angélica and saying straight out, "Look, María Angélica, I'll be home in five minutes," is extremely significant. In one second and for good, it removes all other possibilities. It means committing himself to a certain prearranged plan, embarking on a course he firmly made up his mind about earlier. In other words, doing nothing, letting things stand as they are, and wisely not rocking the boat. And in this simple, apparently banal or arbitrary way, eliminating at one go all vacillation. After which, he's sure, this unfocused fear which keeps turning his legs to jelly will also go away.

He enters the bar, a lot calmer now, and goes to the phone with the solemnity of a person approaching the altar. The altar is not in use, and stepping up to it, Sanctis almost comes to attention, fully aware of the irrevocable step he's beginning to take. The act of making this phone call assumes all the importance of a ritual that must be performed with great ceremony and concentration. Sliding a couple of coins out of his pocket, he deposits them in the slot and listens eagerly for the dial tone. Slowly, keeping his finger in the holes as the dial reverses, he rings his house.

He feels that each of these familiar motions constitutes a clear, undeniable proof that he's come to a decision. All this gives him security. Even his legs seem steady now, firmly planted on the floor.

He finishes dialing the last digit. He waits. Less than two full rings and immediately, by María Angélica's quick, clear "Hello," he realizes that his wife was still awake and close to the phone, maybe even sitting there with her book, just as he left her.

His call does not take María Angélica by surprise. On the contrary. For some reason or other, she was expecting it. But Sanctis is too impatient to find out why, and anyway it can't be very important. Shortly, as soon as he gets home, María Angélica will have plenty of time to tell him. So at last Sanctis is ready to speak the sentence he'd prepared—those few well-chosen words that, acting like a spell, will put an end to all his problems.

"Listen, María Angélica. In a—"

But shit, María Angélica interrupts him in the middle to say lightly, "Ah, good thing you called." And right there, without Sanctis's being able to halt her, she hastens to explain the reason for this unexpected relief his phone call has apparently produced. María Angélica speaks rapidly. She says that Perugia phoned only five minutes before. And when she told him that Sanctis might be dropping in on him, he said what a coincidence, as he wanted to see Sanctis too. Perugia was speaking from the San Carlos over on Zufriategui and Maipú Avenue, and he was going to wait there awhile, hoping they'd meet up.

"He must still be there. Where are you?"

"Well, there more or less," Sanctis answers reluctantly. As a matter of fact, the San Carlos is only some twenty yards away. Just by turning his head he can see its lighted window across the street. "But to tell the truth, I don't feel much like it tonight. It's pretty late. Maybe I'll ring him tomorrow and arrange something for then. And now, listen to me, María Angélica—"

"But if you're all that close, why don't you?" she interrupts him again unwittingly. "See him a little while and find out what he wants." Sanctis can't seem to get her to listen. "Maybe he needs you for something. Anyway, don't stay up too late. You were looking tired tonight. How are you now?"

"Better," Sanctis lies, trying to hide his anger.

"You going, then? I want to know just in case he phones again." María Angélica is cornering him without meaning to.

"Well . . . I don't know." Automatically, he takes a step backward and looks toward the San Carlos. Thinking he sees Perugia's profile next to the window, he corrects himself. "Yes, maybe I will. I might look in and see if he's there. I'll find out what he wants and I'll come straight home. I'm a little tired, really, and I'd rather go to bed early."

"Oh, I know what happens once you and Perugia get together."

"No, no, this time I mean it. Look, María Angélica, I really have to come home, because—" For obvious reasons, he leaves the sentence unfinished. That wasn't what he intended to say, and he is impatient with his own stupidity and the way he keeps getting sidetracked. He still wants to settle things in some fashion, and he's trying to work out just how to commit himself to coming home to María Angélica. What occurs to him is to give himself a time limit—one hour.

"Let's say I'll be there by around one. No later, you can be sure of that."

But María Angélica persists in not believing him. As if things weren't bad enough. She feels she has experience in these matters, and she affectionately pulls his leg. "Look, darling, better not say anything, and that way you won't have to make up any excuses. Bye. Take care. Don't eat anything that doesn't agree with you. I'm going to bed right now."

Sanctis utters a resigned but gloomy "Bye." He hears María Angélica hang up, and for a long time he stands there with the receiver in his hand before he, too, hangs up.

Dragging his feet, he trudges to the door. Someone's getting a kick out of putting the silliest obstacles in his way and not letting him do what he wants, what he really needs to do. In frustration, he's angry with Perugia, with María Angélica, with the whole world. All his sound intention of fixing his movements for the next few hours with a definitive "Look, María Angélica, I'll be home in five minutes" went down the drain thanks to Perugia's ballbreaking phone call.

It's not that he has anything in particular against Perugia. Perugia's not a bad guy after all, and Sanctis has had some good times with him. It's just that he doesn't want to be roaming the streets at this time of night. He has a hunch that so long as he stays out he's running a risk, he's exposed. Running what risk? Exposed to what? Well, to those absurd fluctuations of his will that prevent him from putting into practice what he considers a definitive decision. What he's really afraid of is that as long as he's out on the street, this agony of his (because somehow a name has to be attached to it) could go on and on forever.

So the brilliant idea of phoning was a mistake, one more piece of foolishness among the many he has already committed that night. The sensible thing, he now realizes, would have been to take the bus straight back and be done with it. He shrugs his shoulders, sighs, says to himself so whatcha gonna do, and in resignation crosses the avenue to the San Carlos.

He has no option but to go through with meeting Perugia. Could the timing have been worse? Impossible. Perugia is going to go on about business, football, women, his new house in Vicente López, and about how he's still doing aerobics. Christ, just what Sanctis needs

right now. Oh, well, he hopes that at least the conversation won't go on too long. He'll give it an hour. Because,
naturally, he's not going to tell Perugia anything about
what's taken place that night. Why should he? What can
poor Perugia know about a mess like this? Nothing—
obviously nothing. Perugia's on a different wavelength.

Sanctis moves on. All at once, at the risk of being run
down by a bus, he stops in the middle of Maipú Avenue.
Looking toward the San Carlos's window, he smooths
down a nonexistent mustache. Both actions are evidence
that a new idea is trying to penetrate his mind. Yes, sir,
and the idea is this: Is there really no way of talking to
Perugia about this thing? Who knows? Now and then
fate comes up with an unexpected card. And Perugia,
he's pretty smart, pretty well connected. What if he . . .

CHAPTER XII

In which the killer makes his entrance

The guy sitting by the window is not Marcelo Perugia, and what's more he doesn't resemble him in the least. How funny. To think that in the end Sanctis agreed to this more or less forced and inconvenient meeting only because he thought he saw Perugia's profile in the window of the San Carlos. And not only that, but if he hadn't seen him, if he hadn't been stupidly convinced that this guy with the ruddy face and puffy eyes looking absentmindedly toward the street was Marcelo Perugia, Sanctis surely would not have accepted. In other words, he would have found some way of putting off this tiresome meeting, and right now he'd be sitting in a 68 bus bound for home.

One more blind alley, then. Yes, okay, but look how many of them there have been tonight. Turning down Zufriategui to see if by a lucky chance he'll run across Perugia there, Sanctis quickly starts counting up on his fingers the number of false trails he's followed one after another. The list begins, of course, with Elena Vaccaro's phone call and his mistaken notion that the former fatty was on the make when she appeared in the Renault, continues in the form of various tricks played by his imagination, and culminates in his phone call to María Angélica, which backfired on him. Quite a few, to tell the truth. He wonders, in short, if each of the steps he's taken that night hadn't in some way or other come about as a result of a false trail, a mistake, or a foolish misunderstanding. And he has to admit that that's what seems to have happened. And then it occurs to him that someone, a clever ringmaster, a sly, mocking mind, is mysteriously directing his steps by means of these blind alleys, these mistakes, these misunderstandings.

But the truth is that this latest false step is really funny. Because the guy by the window is fat, bald, and has a mustache, while Perugia is thin, has no mustache, and to top it all he still combs a coquettish lock over his forehead, which gives him the look of an old-time matinee idol. Sanctis doesn't know how he could have made such a blunder. Anyway, he's done it, and better not dwell on it anymore.

He casts an eye quickly along the bar in search of Perugia. Deep down, he hopes not to find him, and while his eyes unenthusiastically roam the place, he sends up a momentous "Pray Allah he's not here." In spite of the faint possibility of enlisting help from Perugia, which Sanctis dreamed up as he crossed Maipú Avenue (was this false trail number fifteen or sixteen?), his intuition tells him that it would be best if Perugia weren't there, or if María Angélica had made a mistake about the place or the time, for then his reluctant promise would be kept by this quick—and for Allah's sake, unsuccessful—glimpse into the San Carlos from outside, and he could catch the first bus home without any burden of remorse.

But there's no way that the sly, mocking ringmaster is going to miss this one—no, never, thinks Sanctis in disappointment. Perugia's there in the San Carlos, all right. Invisible, of course, from where Sanctis first looked—that is, from the sidewalk on the other side of Maipú Avenue—but clearly visible from this window along Zufriategui.

There's nothing he can do, then, but go in. Sanctis checks his watch; unnoticed, time's been flying, and it's now twenty past twelve. Worst luck. He walks back the few yards to the corner and enters the San Carlos.

Without much success, he tries to appear carefree and cheerful. At that moment, Perugia lifts his eyes from his newspaper, spots him, and greets him with a big smile.

Nice guy, this Perugia, with his dapper appearance, his slicked-down lock, his heavy signet ring, his hearty way of getting Sanctis a chair. In spite of the fact that he must be the same age as Sanctis, Perugia still has about him a lot of the bright boy from a poor neighborhood that Sanctis remembers from back in their high school days.

"So it was for real, then, huh?"

"What was?" asks Sanctis, completely baffled.

"What do you think? That you were out for a walk and maybe you'd run into me. I thought I'd put my foot in it, and I tried to play along the best I could. I was just about to leave, in fact."

Only then does Sanctis come down to earth. The famous meeting at the San Carlos was no more than a clever cover-up on Perugia's part, just in case Sanctis had been out on the prowl. And fancy Sanctis having taken it literally—even to the point of postponing his urgent need to go home simply for this masquerade. Yet another false step, then, another cunning ploy of the sly joker, who—it's obvious—is having himself a good time at Sanctis's expense. In other words, the hope—rather naive, he now admits—that Perugia might lend a helping hand and put him in touch with some of his wide net of acquaintances must be part of the same blind alley.

Or not. Maybe this isn't a blind alley. Maybe this is the only thing that isn't blind in the whole farce. Maybe the joker, fate, got a kick out of making him miss the target fifteen or twenty times, only to moor him finally alongside this guardian angel called Marcelo Perugia, the archetypal city slicker, complete with Torino parked somewhere around.

Well, let's see . . . let's see what happens, Sanctis thinks, still distrusting his good fortune, as he takes a seat across from Perugia, lights a cigarette, and with a wave of the hand puts to rest any idea of an assignation.

"What's this? You smoking again?"

"Not really. Just tonight. Problems, you know," Sanctis says, and he thinks that this mention of the word "problems" may be a clever way of getting to the point.

"At work?"

"Well, yes. Sort of."

Maybe the question's come up too quickly. Maybe Sanctis hasn't had time to think how best to present the thorny problem to Perugia. So that the thing stays pretty much where it is, diluted in that "sort of," whose meaning is vast and unspecified.

"If it's money, tell me. You know that . . ." Perugia says, accompanying the words with the rather vulgar gesture of reaching for his checkbook.

"No, that's not really it," Sanctis quickly answers. In spite of Perugia's friendly attitude, Sanctis feels that it's not going to be easy to explain—that is, not without giving away too much about his present predicament or looking like a complete madman or fool.

Just as he did with María Angélica, he decides to kick off with a broad, topical subject—the economic situation, for example. Inflation, the cost of living, things like that.

It is undeniable that Perugia has done pretty well for himself in the last two years. He used to live in the same modest building on Monroe Street where Sanctis still lives and where, for want of something better, a friendship of sorts started up between the two former schoolmates. Perugia suddenly went on to become the owner of a flashy house in Vicente López, near the river. But he's no fool, Sanctis thinks, meaning that he knows what's going on in the country, that he's not twiddling his thumbs, in a word.

He was a onetime follower of Perón. Now his politics are anyone's guess. In point of fact, Sanctis has never much discussed politics with Perugia. It's a matter of sounding him out, then. This is why Sanctis takes great pains to prevent Perugia from launching into the story of his latest conquest, and, without being overly specific about his own opinions, he lets the conversation drift to the present-day economic situation. Sanctis holds that as the current course of events is a more or less wholesale disaster, there is little to argue about—on the contrary, the topic lends itself from the word go to mutual understanding. From the economic situation it's easy to move on to repression, to some new outrage on the part of the regime—such as film censorship—then to paramilitary organizations, to kidnappings, to the atrocities that are being committed by the armed forces, etc. And so, little by little, to arrive at his own case, which is to find out if Perugia has contacts who could deliver Sanctis's life-saving message to Julio Cardini and Bernardo Lipstein.

So far so good. His mind still disturbed by the appalling images that haunted him in his walk along Cabildo, Sanctis, now assuming the role of the injured citizen, expatiates on the intolerable economic chaos. He speaks about the fact that money no longer has any value, about the number of businesses that have gone under, about the proliferation of imported junk. He speaks, in short, about what is common knowledge, about what he knows only too well through his job and what is brought home to him every day by María Angélica.

Perugia listens closely. Then he smiles patronizingly and, very slowly, takes over the conversation. He tries to display an immense knowledge of the subject, speaking

119

about the gross national product, exports, the under-valued dollar, the exchange market, and whatnot. And he ends up making an utterly confounded Sanctis see that things are really a lot better than people suppose, that Sanctis hasn't the least idea of what high-level economic leadership is, that in just a year or two the country is going to become prosperous.

"Remember what I'm telling you. These guys know what they're doing. Don't believe everything you hear."

Sanctis, of course, doesn't try to argue. He knows that Perugia will come up with a pat answer every time. If Sanctis takes exception, Perugia will make him see the advantages that will derive from the fact that service charges on his apartment doubled that same day. These guys with the bulldozer-proof optimism are all alike. And Perugia's been an optimist since the day he was born. That's how it is, old pal. What can you do? There's no point in contradicting him or arguing. Besides, Sanctis knows you don't get anywhere with Perugia that way. The most sensible thing to do, then, is to appear convinced, keep nodding his head in agreement, put on his most credulous expression, and give in.

Afterward, so as to make it clear that the subject of the national economy is closed, Perugia leans back in his chair, yawns, and says, "Yes, sir, that's how it is," meaning absolutely nothing, and he lifts his hand to call the waiter.

Thank goodness the waiter appears at once. Sanctis knows that he must press the advantage of this interruption to approach the subject from the other flank. Letting Perugia talk him into a double Scotch and soda on the rocks instead of coffee, Sanctis asks for another pack of Imparciales, and quickly lays out a new strategy.

The waiter goes off. Before Perugia can grab the deck of cards again, Sanctis, though his strategy is still hasty and incomplete, coolly starts talking.

"Yes, of course. You're right. Sooner or later the economy will straighten out. But there are things, frankly—"

"What things?" asks Perugia, immediately swallowing the bait.

"Well . . . I don't know. The beatings they're dealing out, the repression, the kidnappings. All of a sudden ten guys rush into a house, they steal everything, they hustle the victim off, and bye-bye, nothing's seen, nothing's heard. You think that's right?"

Perugia clicks his tongue. "Come on, pal, come on. It's not all that bad," he says, and deep inside Sanctis is happy. Why? Because it's all too clear that Perugia's fierce optimism derives from sheer ignorance. Not that Sanctis hadn't always known it. The man moves in a circle where no one knows a damn about these things. And to cap it all, there's nothing in the newspapers either. Perugia's out in left field. In other words, Perugia is not the bastard Sanctis thought he was a minute ago. He doesn't really side with these military shits; it's just that in his ignorance he thinks everything's okay, the country's going to pull out of it, and stuff like that. He must be involved in some business deal with the armed forces, that's for sure, because once he gave this to be understood—but that's all. A nice guy like Perugia, who's crazy about a bandleader like Pugliese, who plays a good game of billiards, who just now, with complete spontaneity, offered him money, can't possibly uphold the kind of atrocities that are going on. It's just a matter of putting him straight, then Perugia will react like the decent guy he really is. Of this Sanctis has no doubt.

"Look, Perugia, they're talking about twenty thousand people that have disappeared. This is no joke."

"Who's talking about it?"

You see? You see his sheer ignorance? Sanctis thinks almost joyfully. "Well, people—the League for Human Rights, the families. There must be some truth in it. That's what I say."

"And how many do they claim?" asks Perugia, surely horrified.

"Well, twenty thousand, they claim. Okay, say ten. But still—"

"Twenty thousand, eh?"

"So they say."

"That's nothing."

"Sure, all right, there may be more. I've no idea."

"That's still nothing."

"What do you mean?"

"I say it's a drop in the bucket. Get rid of two hundred thousand and the country'll run like clockwork."

He didn't say this with the face of a hardened criminal. He didn't even raise his voice. He said it the way you'd say they should take Bertoni off the cup team and put in Ardiles. Smiling. Patting down his lock. Ogling the bottom of some woman passing by along Maipú Avenue just then. "Get rid of two hundred thousand."

Sanctis sat speechless. He almost can't believe his ears. He really has nothing to say to the man. Totally at a loss, he thinks, This means Perugia . . . This means this guy . . .

Sanctis feels like getting up and running away. He realizes that any attempt on his part to make Perugia see the monstrousness of what he has just said is going to be pointless. Sanctis looks at him in silence, almost out of curiosity. Like a detective story, it seems. There's the murderer across the table.

Sanctis knew Perugia had business dealings with the military government—that was sure. Sanctis now remembers once hearing Perugia speak of "Charlie," referring to a certain Colonel Bermúdez, with whom he was involved in some deal to do with importing textiles or dyes for textiles. Maybe Sanctis had been thinking about Perugia's rather odd business relations, maybe they were there at the back of Sanctis's mind when it occurred to him that his former neighbor might be able to help. Because a businessman has connections with all kinds of people. Everyone knows that. But Sanctis never imagined, not in a million years, that Perugia's relations with the armed forces were of that nature, that he identified with them, that he not only backed all their brutality but considered it insignificant. That he seriously believed in the necessity of wiping out two hundred thousand guys. My God, what have we come to?

He tries to put an end to this conversation, which is making him feel sick. To his relief, the waiter arrives with their whiskies and the cigarettes. Sanctis believes it's high time to shut Perugia up and change the subject. He turns to look about the place, says that strange as it may seem, it must be a year since he last set foot in the San Carlos, and now he finds it bigger, better, brighter. He asks Perugia if he comes here often.

But Perugia's in no mood for these trite remarks. Carried away by his own words, he's barely aware of the presence of the waiter, who is serving them. He talks about the chaos the country was in years earlier, of the order which "we have achieved" at last. Sanctis must remember that long series of strikes and armed attacks on the army "that made our lives impossible." He talks about that fatal amnesty granted criminal elements who afterward had to be "hunted down again, one by one." He talks about the need for an iron hand. He talks about the minister of the economy, Martínez de Hoz, and General Menéndez, to whom he was introduced a couple of months ago in Río Cuarto and whom Perugia found charming, courteous. The same Menéndez they say had four thousand political prisoners shot. Perugia goes on and on.

In the end, the lucky entrance of two women looking like hookers, who pass close to the two men and sit at a table at the back of the bar, forces Perugia to pause respectfully. Sanctis takes this opportunity to put away his whisky at a single go, to respond to Perugia's look of complicity, and to say the first bit of idiocy that comes to mind about unaccompanied girls at this hour of the night and here are he and Perugia dragging their heels talking about politics.

Then, almost lazily, Sanctis gets up, says he's going to take a leak and that he'll be right back, makes a gesture with his eyes in the direction of the two women, and tells Perugia to keep cool, implying that he's not out for such games tonight and won't be able to play along.

Perugia smiles and happily forgets his harangue. Sanctis is well on his way to the toilets, when Perugia decides he has something to tell Sanctis that can't wait.

"Hey, Sanctis, you know something?"

Sanctis turns, startled. "What's up?"

"My elder boy's got into military school. You remember how lazy he used to be? And now look."

Perugia has the face of a proud father. So much so that Sanctis is forced to make some comment. "Really? That's great." And then, in an ambiguous sort of voice that escapes Perugia, Sanctis adds, "The boy seems to be running on the right track."

To be on the safe side, he doesn't wait for Perugia's reply but makes for the back of the room. Whether because of the whisky or the rubbish he's been forced to listen to, Sanctis feels his face is on fire, as if he had a fever.

He enters the men's room. He takes a long piss and thinks rather childishly how good it would be if all the problems, all the trials and tribulations that afflicted one during the course of the day, all the tripe one's heard that remains fixed in one's mind, could be got rid of as easily as one gets rid of piss into a urinal.

He realizes he needs to cool off a bit. He hangs up his jacket, goes to the washbasin, and splashes water over his face. Finding a paper towel, he slowly dries himself, thinking back as he does so on Perugia's words. It's obviously not going to be easy to shrug them off and wash them down the drain. Perugia's words will stay with him for a long, long time. Like scars, like clinging vermin. The whole thing is a nightmare. Can it be, he wonders, that he, the idiot Francisco Sanctis, and not Perugia, is the one who's been living with his head in the sand all these years? Can it be that a man of Sanctis's age and experience has never realized that there are guys who are mimics, so to speak, who adapt with astonishing ease, who, like corks, always stay afloat no matter what happens? Who in their loves and hates always identify with the loves and hates of those in the driver's seat? Can it be that he has been so amazingly naive as to believe that Perugia, of all people, wasn't one of those, that he could get along with Perugia, and that thanks to his generosity and his many friends, Perugia wouldn't hesitate for a moment to lend him a hand, to help him save the lives of the guys singled out by the intelligence agencies, when the fucking truth of the matter is that all the military's atrocities seem small stuff to this animal Perugia, who, like some medieval fanatic, wants two hundred thousand to be wiped out? Can it be that this windbag is a devoted admirer of Martínez de Hoz and the charming, oh-so-suave General Menéndez?

Isn't all this madness? Isn't this the biggest and dumbest of all Sanctis's mistakes? It sure is the case that he hasn't hit the target once tonight.

He's swiftly passing a comb through his hair in front of the mirror, when he comes to a healthy decision. He'll put an end to this meeting as soon as possible and in any way possible, since it's becoming more and more nauseating all the time. Then he'll make for home. He carefully considers a number of excuses. A headache, tiredness, having to get up early the next day, and so forth.

All at once he is struck by a fear. Perugia seems so involved, so sure of what he's saying, that maybe . . . No, no, no. Sanctis flatly rejects the suspicion. No; no way. It just can't be. How could anybody think that Perugia. . . ? Come on. Are we all crazy, then? Perugia isn't a guy to get mixed up in stuff like that.

Maybe not, but anyway it would be best to stop their conversation here and now. Should one opinion, should one little remark slip out, who knows how this guy would take it, and worse, whom he'd repeat it to.

Once again Sanctis feels fearfully alone. If he felt lonely after he'd talked to María Angélica, now, as a result of this meeting with Perugia, the feeling of loneliness and helplessness has become still more acute, more unbearable. This time he feels cornered, ringed in by uncaring strangers, surrounded by a wall of hideous masks that conceal hundreds of enemies. He wants to go home at once to be done with this nightmare.

He comes out of the men's room trying to look calm.

To reinforce the illusion, he glances toward where the two women are sitting. They're drinking Coca-Cola and smoking languidly at a table up against the back wall.

He then looks toward Perugia, who's waiting for him at the other end of the bar. And only then does he realize what he had caught sight of when he was looking at the women.

He thinks he's hallucinating. He thinks that in his crazy state he's seeing what subconsciously he wants to see. He thinks that sleepiness and tiredness and fear are taking him over, and what he needs is to go to bed, to flake out straight through till noon. Because what he thought he saw a second or two after having turned his head away, he now believes he actually did see there at a table in the corner.

Surreptitiously, he turns his head and has another look. Yes, it's him, or someone who looks just like him. How peculiar. Practically impossible. Because Lucho went out of circulation—he may even be one of those who disappeared—at least a year ago.

And yet . . . That boy partly hidden there behind the pillar, the one with the glasses, necktie, and hair so short it's as if it's just been cut, looks exactly like Lucho, the Fernándezes' elder boy, who once, during a party, snubbed Sanctis when he tried to ask some questions that at the time seemed quite reasonable but that now seem absolutely stupid, and whom María Angélica suspected of being involved in something and who all of a sudden left home. Yeah, sure—thinner, better dressed, more grown up maybe (boys of that age change like mad, as everyone knows), but he'd bet anything it's him.

Sanctis has to force himself to tear his eyes away. He knows that although the boy may very well be the Fernández kid, Sanctis can't do anything just now for elementary security reasons. Perugia—he can see him—is looking this way. To go up to Lucho now would be inviting disaster.

So it's a matter of returning to Perugia's table, convincing him they should leave, and then not coming back into the bar until Sanctis is sure his turncoat friend isn't still lurking about. And only then going to the table at the back and talking to the boy, or at least getting a closer look at him so as to be sure. This, naturally, only if the boy's still there when Sanctis returns. Because there's no guarantee that it will be so easy to convince Perugia, and Sanctis has no intention of carrying on with him until two or three in the morning. So, from here on, everything depends on Sanctis. He'll see what he can do.

Was this the ultimate point of the whole evening, then? reflects Sanctis, a few steps away from Perugia's table. Was each of the moves of the sly, mocking joker aimed not at Marcelo Perugia and his alleged connections (as Sanctis stupidly believed for one moment) but at this chance encounter with the Fernández kid? So that the false trails, the mistakes, the misunderstandings, were nothing but stages along the way, steps obviously needed to bring one to this conclusion?

Sanctis feels that this whole interminable night hasn't

been in vain. He's beginning to suspect that his intense—and perhaps unacknowledged—wish to save two lives, to help Julio Cardini and Bernardo Lipstein escape from the murdering hands of Air Force Intelligence, was what made him go round and round in pointless circles until hitting upon the solution that at long last is right here within reach of his hand. If he hadn't felt troubled and compelled by this wish, he wouldn't have left his house, he wouldn't have agreed to meet Perugia, he wouldn't have committed a single one of the stupid errors he has committed. Instead, he would have stayed home, he would easily have let himself be seduced by María Angélica's sweet, sleepy look, he would have made love beautifully with his wife, and he'd now be sleeping beside her like a person blessed. But then Lucho's miraculous appearance (this brilliant checkmate à la Capablanca) would not have taken place. And the sly joker would have suffered a shameful defeat. Or, what amounts to the same thing, Julio Cardini and Bernardo Lipstein, without a savior to warn them in time, would fall like two cherubs into the hands of the sinister lot in the Ford Falcons, would follow the path to torture and death that many of their friends must be following now.

Remarkably, he no longer feels the anger and resentment toward Perugia that he felt only a short time ago. Now that he views him as a necessary link in this chain that led him to Lucho, Sanctis feels almost grateful to Perugia. Because it's obvious, so he thinks, that without this penultimate link, without the good Perugia and his long-winded harangue in favor of the regime, there would have been no way of coming upon Lucho in this unlikely corner of the San Carlos.

It's clear, then, that fate obeys its own laws, and in the final analysis it does things well. There's no doubting this. Because it's quite obvious that Lucho is the person Sanctis has needed ever since he said goodbye to Elena Vaccaro on Olleros Street. Lucho must belong to some group or other (María Angélica was convinced of it), he must have direct contacts at his disposal, and he would certainly know what to do. Maybe a single phone call, a slip of paper discreetly passed on to a girl friend as she's window-shopping, and the group would immediately take action. Someone would set off at once to a little street in Villa Lugano, to an apartment in Villa Urquiza, and Julio Cardini and Bernardo Lipstein would vanish from their homes, and the outraged crews of the Ford Falcons would find the houses empty. Perfect.

Sanctis returns to his table. He knows that his last few minutes with Perugia will seem endless, but he doesn't want to give himself away by being too hasty. He checks his watch. It's just past one. There really isn't much time, and he must be firm if he doesn't want this to drag out too long.

Perugia, nursing his second whisky, begins telling him—it's long overdue—all about his latest fling. Sanctis knows there's no way of avoiding this, and he pretends to be listening closely, while surreptitiously he glances toward Lucho's table. The boy hasn't moved. Although he's a bit far away, Sanctis can see him clearly. It's got to be him. Those eyeglasses, that way of lighting

131

his cigarette with the match cupped in his hand, that habit of running his hand every so often over his forehead and smoothing his hair. No, there's no doubt, it's Lucho, the Fernándezes' eldest kid.

Lucho, too, seems to be waiting for someone, because he keeps looking from his wristwatch to the door. A girl, perhaps.

He's got to hurry things along with Perugia, then, if he doesn't want Lucho to shove off. But this tale of Perugia's latest conquest—Jesus H. Christ—is never-ending. Sanctis has already had to endure his meeting with the girl in the Café Foro, Perugia's cunning strategy to engage her in conversation; he's had to suffer that part of their conversation and the whole history of her bastard of a husband; Sanctis has had to listen to Perugia describe how incredibly like Lauren Bacall the girl is, her suggestive looks, the shape and size of her tits, his invitation for a drive in the Torino, etc. In other words, the same old story. To Perugia it's the most passionate story in the world, and Sanctis has had to put up with it blow by blow because, after all, a friend is a friend.

But now, while the Torino is silently parked outside a five-star motel in Olivos—in other words, when we've got to the crux of the story—Sanctis thinks he's had enough. He's already listened to everything he's had to hear, and the moment has come to say goodbye.

"Jesus, that's terrific," he tells a jubilant Perugia, who seems prouder of his narrative than of the events it relates.

And in keeping with what he planned in front of the

men's room mirror, Sanctis puts on a headache, over-tiredness, having to get up at the crack of dawn (all strung together, just in case), and calls the waiter. Then, going through all the usual motions of who's going to pay, the two get up and leave.

They walk a few slow blocks along Maipú Avenue, and then along Cabildo to Pico. The most dangerous part is still to come: convincing Perugia that it would be good for Sanctis to go on alone to get over his headache, and so avoid being driven home in the Torino. The jock-eying lasts at least five minutes, but Sanctis finally gets his way. Perugia climbs into his fancy green Torino and takes off.

Also in keeping with his plan, Sanctis lets a minute or two pass in case the old windbag shows any sign of dou-bling back. After a reasonable length of time, Sanctis re-traces his steps and sets off again for the San Carlos.

Oddly enough, he's not in the least afraid that Lucho will have left. The sly joker, fate, so Sanctis thinks, may amuse himself setting traps, but he's not going to go out of his way to do anything foolish.

CHAPTER XIII

In which a colored photo of the TV personalities Susana Jiménez and Pipo Mancera playing Chinese checkers on a bearskin rug under the gaze of a handsome Afghan hound may not be as fatuous as it seems

Yes, sir, the boy's still there.

Maybe life's not so bad after all, thinks Sanctis, as he springs up the steps two at a time and enters the bar.

A boundless joy that seems to burst from his skin, from his hands, has wiped away all his tiredness. He sees Lucho there at the far end of the bar, elbows on a table, smoking, looking toward him, and Sanctis has all he can do not to give himself away and rush up to the boy. How wonderful life is, Sanctis tells himself, how full of surprises, how suddenly, magically, it brings one moments as fabulous as the one he's about to experience. After all his coming and going, after so much difficulty, so much indecision, at last to find the one person who can make proper use of his information. And then, without a moment's delay, to pass it on—that is, to set things in motion, so that this information that's now literally

134

scorching his throat can be turned into something wonderfully alive and useful.

Lucho will probably collapse in surprise—that's more than likely. He'll find it hard believing that a guy like Sanctis, a bookkeeper, an old family friend, a classical music freak, completely out of politics, light-years away from all this mysterious activity that Lucho and his friends are involved in, could make use, just like that, of this scrap of information, of this priceless little group of words and numbers, so that simply by hearing them, memorizing them, and putting them in the hands of the right person, two lives will be saved.

He can foresee that to begin with Lucho will find it pretty odd. He may even put on a blank expression and pretend that none of this has anything to do with him. But the boy's no fool. He may or may not reveal any interest in the matter, but he won't waste time over risky or pointless questions like the ones Sanctis asked Elena Vaccaro. Lucho will surely get the message straightaway, and without hesitation, without even bothering to explain anything to Sanctis, will just do whatever has to be done. In other words, a minute or two more, and the lives of Julio Cardini and Bernardo Lipstein will be out of danger, out of the reach of the bastards who are trying to kidnap and murder them. Doesn't this make you want to rub your hands and shout for joy? Doesn't it make you realize that this whole chaotic night has now served its purpose, and that this mysterious purpose is about to be revealed?

He lets out a "Good for Elenita Vaccaro" that's part gratitude and part a cheer. Because he thinks as he dodges around tables and chairs, heading straight for the corner where he spotted Lucho, that, in point of fact, without Elena Vaccaro and her unquestionable dottiness, without her dotty idea of phoning him at his office that afternoon with the dottiest proposition of them all—"to do something"—none of these wonderful things that are about to take place would have been possible. Neither would there have been all that tiresome wait on the corner of Cabildo and Juramento, nor the driving around in circles in the Renault, nor the problems of conscience, nor the risky conversation with María Angélica, nor the nocturnal stroll along Cabildo with the resulting appearance, or something like it, of Julio Cardini and Bernardo Lipstein in the earthly guise of the two young layabouts (one tall and thin, the other fair with curly hair) glimpsed on Paroissien Street, nor the hasty, foolish decision to phone home, nor, of course, the meeting with Perugia at the San Carlos. But what's also quite certain is that without Elenita Vaccaro there wouldn't have been this unbelievable, providential appearance of Lucho.

"Thanks, sweetheart," he murmurs, mentally sending her a kiss while he's still a few steps away from the boy.

He pauses for a second or two to study him close up. It's him—the Fernández kid. There's no doubt about this at all.

Thinking the boy has seen and recognized him, Sanctis smiles and gives him a little wink by way of greeting.

But the boy—his mind obviously on something else—doesn't return the greeting. He narrows his apparently nearsighted eyes and seems to look beyond Sanctis toward the door. Then, quickly, he lowers his head and begins to read. Glancing at what the boy's looking at (the colored photograph on the cover of the weekly *Gente* is lying face up on the table), Sanctis can't help making a face that implies, shit, the trash young people are into today.

He doesn't seem to know me, Sanctis tells himself, a little put out, and he strides firmly toward the little corner table. Just then, perhaps noticing the cold, distant expression on Lucho's face, Sanctis becomes aware of a new problem, something that hasn't entered his mind until now. What if Lucho doesn't believe him? Or what if the kid doesn't trust him, the way he himself didn't trust Elena Vaccaro? What if, just as Sanctis thought about her at first, the boy thinks he's around the bend and simply ignores him? That would really be a foul-up. Because if that happened the boy wouldn't lift a finger, Julio Cardini and Bernardo Lipstein would fall straight into the hands of the intelligence agencies, and then none of the events of this night would make sense. Aw, shit, kid, stop fooling around and listen to me; this thing's serious and we haven't much time, he begs Lucho under his breath as he comes up to him.

"Hello," says Sanctis in a low voice, leaning over the boy slightly.

Lucho lifts his head, a bit startled. He turns pale, and his hand, resting on the table beside a pack of Jockeys and a key ring, begins to tremble. He can't or he won't speak. Staring up at Sanctis, he wrinkles his brow in an almost hostile expression of surprise and discomfort.

"Don't you remember me? I'm Sanctis, your father's friend. We've seen each other several times at your house," and he finishes the sentence with a fairly cheerful, confidence-boosting, "How are you?"

"Ah, yes," the boy says finally, with a slurred, adenoidal twang. "I thought I knew you, but I couldn't remember where from."

And that's all. Not another word. He doesn't invite Sanctis to sit down. He makes a slight, cold response to Sanctis's gesture, holding out a soft, reluctant hand.

The boy's waiting for someone, Sanctis tells himself, and his own presence must be inconvenient. Yes, all right, but Sanctis is fully aware of what's at stake at this moment (the lives of two guys, damn it), and even if this meeting's going nowhere, Sanctis isn't about to give up now just because of Lucho's unhelpful spoiled-brat attitude.

In a firm but friendly voice, Sanctis says, "Listen to me. I'm not going to take up more than a couple of minutes of your time. May I?"

He takes a chair and sits down opposite Lucho. To be sure they won't be overheard, he peers around. He sees a man going up to the girls' table, a big dark guy in a gray suit, who greets them with a pat on the back. The man stands there smiling, chewing gum, and saying something no doubt very funny, because the girls' shrieks of laughter can be heard everywhere. The guy looks like a plainclothes cop, and—just in case—Sanctis decides to speed things up.

Lucho has neither accepted nor rejected Sanctis's proposal to join him. Instead, he pretends to be looking at the time and gives a curt—though perhaps unintentionally so—shrug of resignation. Then, with a habitual nervous movement rather like a tic, he raises his glasses, rubs his eyelids, passes his hand over his forehead and hair, and ends up lighting a cigarette with a match cupped in his hand. He does not offer Sanctis one.

Sanctis looks him over closely. The kid is definitely thinner than the last time they met. He's really emaciated and has dark circles under his eyes, as if he's just got over a bout of flu. Though from afar he seemed better dressed than usual, perhaps owing to his necktie and the recent haircut, now, up close, his collar looks dirty and crumpled, as if he hadn't changed his shirt for several days. He frequently clears his throat, and from time to time he presses a tattered handkerchief to his mouth. He looks ill, and Sanctis can't help but ask him what's the matter.

"Nothing. What do you mean?" Lucho answers defensively.

Now Sanctis notices that the boy has several rotten teeth. Perhaps that's why he speaks little—and then without moving his lips. Sanctis also notices the eyes red from lack of sleep, the shifty look, the shaking hand that holds the cigarette, the bad skin color. How different from the self-confident, smiling Lucho who used to appear in the Fernández little living room on his way back from school or a basketball game.

"Well, I don't know . . . I just thought," Sanctis says in a conciliatory way. "But don't worry, I'm not going to ask any questions."

Sanctis is beginning to get some idea of what's been going on with the boy. But even so, even if Lucho's having a rather bad time, Sanctis must still press him and pass on the message.

"Aren't you?" says Lucho vaguely, shifting his legs impatiently and glancing toward the door.

"No," answers Sanctis dryly. "I came to tell you something."

He takes a paper napkin and quickly jots down two names and addresses. Then, turning the slip around, he pushes it across the Formica, and leaves it squarely in front of Lucho. He waits a second or two. Then, in a voice that he tries to keep unemotional, Sanctis says, "They're coming for them tonight." The knowledge that he's just repeated Elena Vaccaro's exact words makes him smile.

Lucho appears not to understand a thing. Without troubling to pick up the napkin, he reads what's in front of him but says nothing. He shows no surprise. He shows—Sanctis can hardly believe it—no emotion at all. When Lucho finishes reading, he turns his tired eyes on Sanctis, clears his throat, and brushes the paper away as if to say, "So what? These things happen all the time. What are we supposed to do?"

Sanctis is still expecting Lucho to react. Since the boy hasn't spoken, Sanctis looks at a clock up over the bar. It's already twenty to two; he's beginning to run out of patience. He tries to keep his voice low, but anger creeps in, and he presses. "You haven't understood me, Lucho. I told you they're coming for them tonight. I mean Air Force Intelligence. There's still time to act. Don't you realize? Listen to me. Don't be thick."

Lucho nods his head like a boy who's been ticked off. But that's all. He's not making any decision, he's not saying a word, and, goddamn it, he doesn't even seem to have understood. He just stares at Sanctis, thinking of God knows what, his eyes vacant, until his gaze shifts again to some mysterious spot behind Sanctis's back. Sanctis then begins to scrutinize this frightened, exhausted seventeen-year-old who's waiting for something, his nerves on edge, in this bar on Maipú Avenue at two o'clock in the morning. And all at once Sanctis feels a wave of pity for the boy, a sort of tenderness, a need to give him courage, the way one would feel about any poor helpless kid at the end of his tether and beset by the whole world. He regrets having called him thick. Now that Sanctis sees him here, it's easy to imagine what Lucho's been through, what he's going through now: the friends he must have lost, his loneliness, the stresses and strains of a life in hiding. This whole year has been tough on these kids, Sanctis thinks. Defeated, hunted down like criminals, murdered. Shit, who can ask Lucho, played out as he is, to do any more than he's already doing? After all, he's let Sanctis sit at his table, listened to him, and although his mind is obviously elsewhere, the boy is trying to keep up appearances, to show the rudiments of decent behavior despite his impoliteness of a few minutes ago. Considering Lucho's all-but-impossible position, no one can demand more of him.

Yes, of course, all this is true. But that's no reason to get deflected now. Nor is there any question but that what Sanctis has to reveal will lose all significance in this mood of gloom or depression that holds Lucho in its grip. The events of this long shambles of a night will have been squandered in a pointless, foolish wandering from streets to bars simply because the boy, up to his neck in his own problems, can't bring himself to pass on a scrap of paper—the very minimum that must be done to keep two guys from falling into the wrong hands. No, sir, this just can't be. Sanctis cannot give in to this abject failure, and, with heavy insistence, he tries again.

Taking the boy by the arm, he shakes him, trying to get a reaction out of him, trying to break through that shell of indifference or distrust into which Lucho seems to have withdrawn.

"Listen to me, kid. This is important, goddamn it. You've got to believe me. For God's sake, Lucho, pay me a bit of attention."

Lucho gives a start. Beneath the boy's clothes Sanctis feels the tense muscles of a cornered animal. The boy stares at him with a mixture of fear, hate, and supplication. His eyes are telling Sanctis to leave him alone, to go away, not to get mixed up in his life, not to pester him anymore.

Sanctis understands the look perfectly, and it dawns on him that in the kid's present state he can't be counted on to make decisions. Sanctis leans toward Lucho, speaks to him in a friendly, reassuring way, which, unwittingly, has a paternal touch about it. The fact is that Sanctis has almost forgotten why he came to sit here at this table. Now, face to face with Lucho, he can't think of anything else but this boy, on the run, underfed, scraping along, the remnant not of a defeat but of a carnage, and obviously in need of help.

"It's all right," he says to him. "Don't tell me anything you don't want to. Let me know if you need anything, if I can do anything for you."

Sanctis is trying to lift his spirits, asking Lucho to trust him, and says, "You see, Lucho, all this will pass." He wants the boy to understand that he must trust someone, and in assuring Lucho that anything he says won't go any farther, Sanctis becomes emotional to the point of foolishness.

"You know I'm a friend of your parents, so I'm not going to do anything to cause you trouble. Let me know if I can give you a hand. That's all."

Perhaps it was the moving sincerity that the boy sensed in Sanctis's words. Perhaps his tense nerves relaxed suddenly on hearing this man, who was a lot like his father, who must have some imagination but who could have no idea what Lucho's life had been over these past months, and who was naively trying to help him. Perhaps after such long silence, after constantly being on the lookout and in danger, Lucho needs to speak to someone, to tell someone about this dreadful time he's been through, for which he cannot have been prepared, and the signs of which are only too evident in his face. And then this guy, his father's friend—and so like his father—suddenly becomes the friend he lacks, the confessor, the repository for all the horror Lucho bears within him and needs to let out, if just this once. The fact is that Lucho will soon give in quite naturally and without resisting or taking up a stance. Little by little, the barriers behind which he took refuge have been falling, his look becomes less hard, less shifty, his teeth unclench, and he begins to speak.

He doesn't say much, of course. Barely a few dry, broken sentences, interspersed with long pauses during which he seems to hesitate and to wonder whether he's doing the right thing. Barely a passing reference to his isolation, "cut off completely," he says, for over the past two months; to friends dead or disappeared, "my whole group," he says; to some leader whom he's suddenly stopped seeing, who "stopped going to meetings," and who, as he later found out, left the country without telling anyone; to the many places he's been living in over the past year, places "he had to clear out of" usually a few days or hours before "they were raided," as a result of which he's still alive, "by pure chance," he says.

Sanctis hears about this unfamiliar world, whose existence in the labyrinth of his own city he barely suspected and that now takes shape before his eyes through the few words—full of drama, despair, and horror—that Lucho manages to utter.

So this is one of the two hundred thousand who have to be wiped out, Sanctis thinks in sorrow, in irony, and

144

with a tremendous urge to remove himself forever from this lousy world where boyhood friends—nice warm guys—are possessed with the violent desire to kill two hundred thousand people, and where boys like this one sitting here seem to have no place and are hunted down and killed like prey.

"So I left the last house three days ago," says Lucho, concluding.

"And where've you been sleeping these last three nights?" Sanctis asks with an instinctive, almost motherly concern.

"I don't know—bars, trains, buses. In fact, I haven't slept."

And seeing Sanctis put his hand over the annotated napkin and slowly pull it back toward himself, Lucho says by way of excuse or explanation, "I'm in no state to save anyone, don't you see? I see no one. I've no contacts. I'm completely cut off—that's the truth of it."

Sanctis nods his head to show he understands, he does see. He understands everything or nearly everything. He at last understands Lucho's true predicament. He realizes that what he imagined or hoped for is going to be impossible. He stares pensively off to one side, and all at once begins speaking casually again, as if trying to change the subject and take pressure off the boy.

"What are you doing around here?"

Lucho hesitates for several seconds. "I'm waiting for papers to get out of the country," he says at last. "Some guy's bringing them to me." He looks at the time and adds, "That's what he said, anyway."

Sanctis then has an idea which seems to be the great solution. He sees a germ of hope, and he says, smiling and pointing at the napkin, "Listen. This guy's that's coming—couldn't he . . . ?"

"No." Lucho's reply is decisive.

"Why not?"

"Because."

He gives no explanation, and Sanctis decides that this mysterious person who's coming either isn't a friend of Lucho's or is someone Lucho doesn't trust. Anyway, Sanctis realizes he mustn't ask any more questions.

"He should have been here by now," says Lucho, glancing toward the door for the hundredth time.

Sanctis looks too. Trusting his own eyes more than Lucho's, he asks, "What's he look like?"

"I don't know. He has to spot me."

"Does he know you?"

"No, he doesn't. He'll know me by these," he says, pointing to the copy of *Gente,* the pack of Jockeys, and the key ring. "That's why I must be alone, understand?"

Sanctis, who has just come to grips with youth and its edifying reading matter, says yes, he understands, and in a second he'll leave Lucho alone. With a swift movement, Sanctis presses into Lucho's hand almost all the pesos he has in his wallet, insisting that the boy take them.

After a moment's hesitation, Lucho accepts.

"I don't know when I'll be able to pay you back," he says, and in gratitude he touches Sanctis lightly on the arm.

146

"Do you need anything else?"

"No—really. The best thing's to leave me alone now."

"Have you somewhere to go?"

"If the guy shows up, I'll take the next bus to Brazil. Everything's just about arranged."

"What if he doesn't turn up?"

"If he doesn't, I don't know."

Sanctis is about to say something, but he thinks better of it and remains silent. He remembers his conversation with María Angélica earlier on, he remembers what he himself said very firmly about the impossibility of keeping anyone, even a friend, hidden in the apartment. He remembers what he said about the danger that put everyone in. Now, rubbing a hand vigorously over his face, he says, "Come to my house."

To justify this to María Angélica, he tells himself that if she'd been there and seen the Fernández boy the way Sanctis is seeing him, she would have done the same thing.

Only then perhaps does Sanctis become fully aware of his own predicament. He picks up the napkin, holds it between two fingers, and puts a match to it. The last blind alley, he thinks with a mixture of irony and bitterness, watching the bit of paper burn to ash.

Laboriously, he gets to his feet. He feels tired again. Leaning his hands on the table, he says these last words to Lucho in a low voice: "I'm going to wait outside just by the door. If the guy doesn't show up, you come that way and we'll go home together, okay?"

"Okay," answers Lucho.

Sanctis takes leave of him with a "Good luck" and a wink, which this time Lucho responds to with the wisp of a smile. Then Sanctis makes slowly for the door.

He leaves the San Carlos, takes a few steps toward the curb, and stands there as if waiting for a bus. Glancing furtively back into the bar, he can see Lucho and a few yards away from him the guy in the gray suit, who's now sitting at the girls' table. A sudden fear comes over Sanctis. What if this is a trap? What if this gorilla is in league with the guy coming to meet Lucho, and they plan to nab the kid there in the San Carlos?

The most sensible thing would be to stand on the opposite sidewalk or at the corner, but not here where they'd probably grab him too. But Sanctis is too tired, and out of sheer inertia he doesn't move a step.

The minutes drag interminably. Finally he sees someone come out of the men's room and go up to Lucho's table. He has long hair, and is wearing jeans and a checked shirt. He sits down across from Lucho and places a folded newspaper on the table.

"Thank goodness," says Sanctis with a sigh of relief, looking automatically at his watch. It's past two o'clock.

CHAPTER XIV

In which Muammar Qaddafi and a certain ramshackle old number 28 bus come to play an unexpected role, and also in which, amidst panting and gasping, we hear the cabalistic, semantically ambiguous words "to the end of the line"

Suppose Francisco Sanctis's story were to stop right here. Suppose that at the exact moment Sanctis said, "Thank goodness," sighed with relief, and cast a heedless glance at his watch, the end had come. If you think about it, nothing could be more logical. The inner conflict, or moral dilemma, that has been the subject matter of this tale, and whose convolutions we have followed through thirteen intricate chapters, no longer lacks a solution. For better or for worse, despite the absence of major incidents or blinding revelations on the road to Damascus, perhaps without ever having come to a hard-and-fast decision, Sanctis has been trying for some time (quite ineffectively, it is true, and with invariable bad luck) to save the lives of two men whom the whims of fate have put into his hands. What more can we expect of him? The personal wrestling match is over, no equivocation remains, and so the story that began at five o'clock in the afternoon on Friday the eleventh of November 1977, with a telephone call from a former fat girl is almost played out. From now on, we should be able to dispense with the moral dilemma encountered on page one, to whose gradual resolution we've been almost unwitting onlookers.

All this is undeniable, but there are other reasons for wanting the story to end here and now. We might want Sanctis to realize that it's very late, for example, and that this is no time for traipsing about the streets like a lost soul. We are in Buenos Aires, in 1977, at the height of the repression, and everyone wants to keep out of trouble. The less a man is seen alone in the streets at two o'clock in the morning, the better. We might want to witness Sanctis at last make for the safety of María Angélica's arms, for she's probably wondering where on earth he can be.

We promise, therefore, not to go on too much more, and only for the sake of coherence shall we spin the story out a little longer by returning to Francisco Sanctis, who is still standing there just outside the San Carlos, nearly wiped out with exhaustion, rooted to the spot, apparently unable to make up his mind to step down off the curb and undertake the dizzying voyage across Maipú Avenue to catch his bus.

It should be pointed out that more than ever, more than at any point during this night, he feels totally alone. The city is a sprawling desert in which the few people still wandering about can only be ghosts, strange indifferent beings whom it is not only forbidden but also quite possibly dangerous to accost. The last shred of hope, which literally kept him together (the Lucho solution), vanished like the cigarette smoke above the tables in the San Carlos, and the image of the Fernández boy, whom Sanctis can still see at the far end of the bar, has left him aching with defeat and impotence.

It's as if the world were deliberately moving away from him. He feels forsaken, alienated, floundering in the middle of this night that has no beginning and no end.

Perhaps in a vague effort to escape temporarily this eerie feeling of detachment, of unreality, which has made him, too, feel a kind of ghost, he tries desperately to cling to the everyday things around him. He stares at a sidewalk tile. It's filthy, one corner is cracked, and the neon blaze from the San Carlos throws strange shadows over it. Next his eyes light on a gray car that speeds past, entering the huge shadowy maw of the Puente Saavedra underpass, and emerges again on the other side, tiny in the lights of Cabildo. He listens hard to the sound of a small brown beetle bumping against the lighted windowpane, and he studies it as it lies squirming on its back on the doorstep. He hears a police siren a long way off, a train pulling away from a nearby station.

He tries to work up a reaction. He tells himself that this feeling of not being there, of having fled from the face of the earth, must come from tiredness. He tells himself that if he goes on being obsessed by trivia, he's really going to crack.

He gazes up at the star-studded sky over Maipú Avenue. To revive himself, he takes a deep breath, and at the same time spits out a low-voiced "Son of a bitch," aimed vaguely at his dismal feeling of alienation, at the government, at Air Force Intelligence, at the sinister series of false trails he has followed, at the world in general, and at all these things put together.

The feeble exorcism must have worked, because after shaking his head to clear it, Sanctis at last withdraws one foot from the curb, then the other, and ventures slowly across Maipú Avenue.

Although he ignores the traffic light flashing "Don't Walk," his guardian angel protects him and delivers him safe and sound on the other side, where he can catch his bus.

Immersed in his thoughts and paying no heed to what he's doing, he leans against a signpost and lights a cigarette. He wants a second or two of peace, he wants to think a little, to turn things over in his mind, to try to understand something of what's taken place that night. But his thoughts never even begin to take shape. They dissolve, one in the other, like water in water. The images in his mind blend with what he is seeing in the street, with the toe of his shoe, which for a moment becomes the most significant object in the world. He has no idea what he's going to do in the next five minutes. He has no strength to make any decision. Strangely enough, he's in no hurry to return to María Angélica. He has only the hazy idea that sooner or later he'll have to catch a bus and get off at Monroe Street. He just stands there. He smokes, half closing his eyes. For a fraction of a second he may even have fallen asleep.

His mind is blank. And yet it's at this very moment that two rather odd things happen, which should be faithfully recorded because, as will be seen, they are going to cause the end of this story to be deferred for a few more pages.

First, a driver on the number 60 bus (a shock-headed, villainous-looking character, resembling Muammar Qaddafi) comes bowling at full speed down Maipú Avenue. Spotting Sanctis propped against the post from a hundred yards off, and although he's not been flagged down, he takes it into his scruffy head that the man planted there must be waiting for his bus. Then something scarcely credible happens. Carried away by a mood of rare compassion, Scruff slips deliberately into neutral, jams on the brakes, and coasts—yes, sir, elegantly coasts—his mastodon to the curb, as stately and inviting as a tame camel of the desert, six inches from where Sanctis stands. The driver then turns his head, and with a dusky, paternal look orders his poor strayed sheep to climb aboard.

Taken completely by surprise, Sanctis is about to stub out the cigarette he's just lit and obey without a peep, but at the last moment, for reasons that he himself could not have explained, he shakes his head, turns on his protector and shepherd of souls a face full of humble apology, and not shifting his feet, looks toward the far end of Maipú Avenue as if waiting for another—nonexistent—bus.

The driver stares Sanctis up and down in disgust and indignation, as though fate were trying to palm off on him—Qaddafi—the most loathsome of traitors. Spitting on the sidewalk, he rams the bus into first, and hurls at Sanctis (and at all half-wits, bastards, and perverts running loose on the streets at this time of night) the longest, most descriptive, most unforgettable of oaths.

Second, while the final echoes of the oath are still audible from half a dozen blocks away, the last number 28 bus (Estación Saavedra to Puente Uriburu), a peeling, wheezy old rattletrap, still miraculously in service, splutters laboriously out of the darkness of a side street. First gear slips, the bus lurches forward a few yards in a series of coughs, fits, and starts. Back in elusive first gear, it sticks its hesitant muzzle out into Maipú Avenue.

This contraption bears no likeness whatsoever to the brand-new buses with tasteful upholstery and quiet motors that power their way up and down Cabildo. Nevertheless, as if boarding this prime heap of junk had suddenly become his dearest ambition, Sanctis heaves himself off the post without a moment's delay, and runs like a maniac to try to clamber on.

He skirts a pillar, comes within an inch of the murderous edge of a metal newspaper kiosk temporarily abandoned by its owner, El Tipo de Puente Saavedra, reaches the side street at surprising speed, and in a smart diagonal trotting step worthy of the cream of the old-time news vendors, he manages to draw level with the old heap's door. Placing both hands on the grab bars, he takes a flying leap and somehow or other manages to land inside the darkened bus.

When in a drowsy voice the driver asks, "Where to?" Sanctis has to pause, waiting to catch his breath. Even then he can only pant and gasp out, "To the . . . to the end of the line."

CHAPTER XV

In which Cerberus installs himself in the middle of Lacarra Street barking his three heads off, the river Styx comes slap up against an arsenal, and Charon, who hails from Villa Alberdi, in the northern province of Tucumán, asks bluntly, "Where are you going, brother!"—all of which leads us to suspect that matters have gone beyond a joke

This Bernardo Lipstein seemed so tough and brawny as he leaned against the post on Paroissien Street whispering to Julio Cardini. Now, here in his bungalow on Lacarra Street (where Lipstein let him in when Sanctis clapped his hands to announce his arrival), seeing him up close as he sits on a kitchen stool, elbows propped on the blue oilcloth of the table, it's incredible but he looks a wreck—thin as a slab of dried cod, pallid, unsteady, his fingers yellow from smoking too much, and his shirt collar frayed and grimy.

The man keeps glancing toward the door as he tells Sanctis in a thick, congested voice that he recognizes him but doesn't remember from where. Then he falls silent, lost in thought, running a hand over his forehead and through his blond curls. When he gets up, he makes a sign to Sanctis that he'll be right back, and begins rummaging in a drawer in search of a colored photograph of Susana Jiménez, without which, as everyone knows, it's absolutely impossible to leave the country. But interrupted suddenly, the man lifts his head, transfixed, his face frozen in terror. The voice of the guy in the gray suit can be heard out beyond the open window, telling the two hookers a very funny story, so funny that when he delivers the punch line—"Liniers Station!"—the girls collapse, and their shrill laughter begins rattling all the glasses and plates and cutlery. Sanctis struggles to open his eyes.

He finds himself curled up on the back seat of the bus, beside the window. His neck aches, his mouth is dry, and his sweaty shirt clings to him.

A few seconds pass before he grasps the fact that the bus is the number 28, that the narrow asphalt strip up ahead is General Paz Avenue, that the window his head is still leaning against looks out beyond the city limits at the built-up suburbs of the Province of Buenos Aires.

Without stirring from his uncomfortable position, and with as much desire to reestablish contact with the world as to undergo a gall bladder operation, Sanctis peers around him, bleary-eyed. Somehow it's like peering through a dirty windowpane or a mosquito net. After a series of jerks and thuds, the bus whines to a halt at the stop for Liniers. Sanctis sees the back of a thin man in a hat, who gets up and moves toward the door carrying a guitar case under his arm; he sees two guys (possibly night-shift workers) get on, pay their fares, and sit together in silence in the second row; he sees the back of the head of a man asleep two rows in front of him; and while he's looking, the head suddenly and convincingly turns into a red sweater, beneath which two tremendous worlds in expansion swell and throb, and next a huge smiling face draws closer, closer, almost to the point where a tuft of lank hair touches him, filling him with a crawling sensation of revulsion. Realizing he's on the verge of falling dead asleep, he makes one last heroic effort to sit up straight in the seat, stretches, rubs his eyes, smooths down his hair, and lights a cigarette.

With the first couple of drags he begins sizing up his situation, which is (1) that he's where he is because a short time earlier, owing to an impulse as sudden and crazy as any he's had that night, he decided he couldn't let the last 28 bus from Puente Saavedra to Pompeya pass him by; (2) that, consequently, he's heading, not only without a specific plan but in the most slapdash way, to the 4200 block of Lacarra Street; (3) that quite possibly he's embarking on the greatest blunder of his life; and (4) that this draft coming up through the floorboards of the bus, creeping up his trouser legs, and milling about in the region of his stomach is no draft really but his old pal the jitters.

He wonders whether this little outing to Villa Soldati is the cause of his fear, and he has to admit it isn't. A journey like this one, surely pointless and undertaken at two o'clock in the morning, couldn't possibly scare anyone. Why not? Because what Sanctis is doing, being the

157

result of neither a long-range plan nor some brave, spur-of-the-moment decision to save a man's life by risking his own neck, is about as dangerous as a stroll through Palermo Park on a Sunday afternoon.

All right, quite true, he tells himself, so what's this little trip about, then? He wants to give himself a reasonable answer, but the horrendous rattling of the bus (which has now managed to summon up power and is barreling along General Paz between the outlying sections of Mataderos and La Matanza) reverberates through his body, confusing and distracting him. In time to the unbearable racket, his thoughts shake and bounce around in his skull, blending like liquids in a cocktail shaker. So, what with squeaky springs, the stentorian rattle of loose windows, and the wheezing and gasping of the engine, when he asks himself where on earth he's going, and what in hell he'll do when the bus reaches goddamn Lacarra Street, he holds out little hope of an intelligent answer.

Most likely, he figures, he'll just get off at the corner. Okay, and what next? Well, next he'll walk slowly and nonchalantly till he comes to the 4200 block. And then? And then, from the sidewalk, without stopping, he'll shoot a sidelong glance at number 4225. And then? And then probably he'll turn right around, pass the house again, and keep going—or will leave a note, or will ring the bell, or rather will knock once or twice and see what happens, or . . .

Suddenly he jams the brakes on his imagination and comes down to earth. Where do these crazy notions stem from? It's beyond anything even Elenita Vaccaro might have dreamed up, and Sanctis is convinced that all he's been thinking is sheer nonsense, that he still has time to backtrack, and that it would be good not to add another stupid thing to those he's already done that night.

Adding insult to injury, on passing Avenida del Trabajo, the street name, glimpsed out of the corner of his eye, reminds him of his job and his comfortable office overlooking Avenida de Mayo. Then of the list of credits outstanding he plans to have ready for Monday afternoon, of the pleasant smell of coffee coming up from the storeroom, of Monsreal's Catalan accent, of the switchboard operator's legs, of five o'clock quitting time, when the bell rings, of the bronze horses outside the Capitol spouting water, of the journey home on the number 60 bus. And on the spot he's overcome with a tremendous urge to hurl himself off this particular bus, the 28, and fly through the air back to Belgrano, take refuge in his apartment, and give up all thought of this expedition to the hinterlands of Villa Soldati—an expedition he can no longer make head or tail of.

But he doesn't do so, for two reasons. First, because God knows how he'd ever get from Mataderos all the way to Belgrano at this time of night. And second, because every bone in his body aches, his feet are so swollen he's had to untie his shoes, and just the thought of lifting his butt off the seat exhausts him.

As a small consolation, he tells himself he can get off this bus anytime he feels like it, there's no reason at all to feel scared, and besides, up till now he hasn't done a thing—hasn't made the ghost of a move—that could be considered dangerous.

Again he rests his head against the window, smokes, stares at the strange shadows that race along the aisle, vaulting the seats and the backs of the seats, every time the bus passes under a street lamp. He observes how the shadows start backward at first, as if about to take a run, and then charge wildly forward, fleeing in fear from the bus and hurtling to meet the next lamp, as if wanting to proclaim in advance the rattletrap's late but unfailing arrival. It's probably the result of studying these fanciful shadows advancing like phantoms ahead of the objects that produce them that sets Sanctis playing with or being carried away by some whimsical ideas about fatalism, predestination, omens, and such—notions that may derive from his years at the seminary and that crop up unexpectedly from time to time in the Sanctis of November 1977, who tends toward the metaphysical and is certainly more religious-minded than he imagines.

He asks himself, for example, if this trip he's now making was in any way planned or foreseen (foretold, would be better) each step of the way since he said goodbye to María Angélica at around eleven o'clock and set off (without the slightest hesitation, he now sees) toward Puente Saavedra. If everything that's happened to him since then—all the false trails, all the blocks he's walked, all the apparently pointless meetings, etc.— were only preparatory steps, a prologue, so to speak, warming-up exercises for undertaking this unbelievable and (for mortals) unpredictable journey. So that in the same way and with the same precision that the passing of the bus is foretold by the hurtling shadow that precedes it, was not this journey already laid down, foreshadowed, in him?

All at once he shakes his head and scolds himself that he's thinking rubbish, that these would-be dotty or abstract happenings are products of exhaustion and the fact of doing nothing but watching a long string of street lights whizzing by. In the final analysis, if he caught this old heap at Puente Saavedra it was simply because it was there under his nose, and it seemed a pity to miss the last bus to Puente Uriburu. That's all there was to it—the sort of thing that can happen to anyone—so there's no need to get worked up trying to find obscure reasons for such a simple action.

In an effort to convince himself of this, and also to stop himself from thinking wild thoughts, he decides to kill these last few minutes before reaching his destination by doing something specific and possibly more useful. He'll study each of his traveling companions.

He counts them. They are five. The driver; another driver coming off work, who stands on the step just inside the door; the night-shift workers, who are now talking in low voices; and the guy with his head on his chest, whose back view a few moments ago underwent a frightening transformation. Sanctis looks them over, makes what he considers a sharp deduction, and decides that none of them is a plainclothes cop. And the funny part is that this on-the-spot evaluation, arrived at hastily and without any real basis, has the extraordinary power of lifting him into a limbo of peace.

The bus is now crossing over the highway to Ezeiza. Sanctis, who owing to this newfound peace is afraid of falling asleep again, opens the window. A cool gust blows straight into his face, and he half closes his eyes, gulping in the wind and savoring its restorative massage. He also hears the unexpected sound of crickets and smells newly mown grass, open countryside, and damp earth. He takes several deep breaths and feels better.

Soon after they pass the Ezeiza road, Sanctis's mind conjures up the series of gruesome pictures (weed-choked plots, corpses with their hands tied behind their backs, empty cartridges, etc.) that for some time now he's associated with the word "Ezeiza," particularly on reading the newspapers. He feels cold; he also feels a shiver down the spine that has nothing to do with the cold. He sees himself thrown into a field, face down on the ground, his riddled body between the bodies of Julio Cardini and Bernardo Lipstein, also savagely filled with holes. At once he thinks of Him who preached in Galilee, who was tortured and killed and whose body was displayed as a warning to others between the racked bodies of two guys he didn't even know. Sanctis cannot shake off a deep sentiment that's tinged oddly with resignation and comfort.

But the resignation and comfort go rapidly to hell when in his morbid imagination he sees María Angélica by the living-room lamp, her glasses slipped down on her nose, reading the evening paper and suddenly coming across the headline "Grim Discovery." He squirms to see González promoted to head of department and occupying—bastard that he is—Sanctis's desk with the view of Avenida de Mayo.

Luckily, the bus is coming to Puente de la Noria, so it can't be far to Lacarra. Sanctis has to cut off the tearful account of his death in the middle (just as Elena Vaccaro, veiled in black, surreptitiously approaches the candlelit coffin, laying on it a big spray of red carnations), because from here on, if he doesn't want to miss his stop, he's got to pay attention to the street signs.

At the Puente de la Noria turnoff, the sleeping man comes to, looks out in bafflement, and shouts to the driver to stop right there. Then he rushes out, obviously a long way past the place he intended to get off.

Sanctis knows the bus will now head down a narrow roadway parallel to the watercourse of the Riachuelo, and at some point they'll cross Lacarra Street. Making himself ready, he ties his shoes, gets up, and moves to the front seat. Surprising himself by the calmness of his voice, he asks the driver for Lacarra Street.

Somehow, the act of uttering the prohibited words aloud for the first time gives Sanctis a boost of confidence. At last, openly and without subterfuge, he's spoken to a complete stranger about hitherto unmentionable Lacarra Street. Sanctis is turning into a man of action. But the driver, pig that he is, shoots down all Sanctis's intrepidness when he grunts out a curt and scarcely audible "Still a way to go" that seems directed more to the gear lever or to his ticket machine than to his passenger.

Just then, however, over the shoulder of one of the night-shift workers, now sitting just behind Sanctis, an angel of compassion descends, whispering into the man's ear in a language that might be either German or Polish, "Lean forward and say to the gentleman who asked the question that you'll let him know exactly when the bus reaches Lacarra." Obeying, the night-shift worker leans forward, and in an accent that could be either German or Polish, he utters these two blessed words: "I tell."

Sanctis turns. His benefactor, a fair-haired man with sunken cheeks and several days' stubble, barely responds to Sanctis's smile but makes a sign with his hand that gives Sanctis to understand he shouldn't worry, he'll be told when to get off.

Sanctis expresses his thanks and, secure in the knowledge that he's temporarily under the blond man's wing, he devotes himself, almost with the curiosity of a tourist, to gazing out the window.

This narrow way along which the old rattletrap is bucketing seems to be called, for no reason Sanctis knows, 27 de Febrero Street. He also discovers that this revolting smell he's been aware of for some time now stems from the surroundings—one endless garbage dump, mile after mile of it, stretching along either bank of the Riachuelo.

The landscape, to tell the unvarnished truth, is gloomy. Mounds of refuse receding into infinity; the stinking canal, now like a filthy sewer, and making Sanctis feel like one of the cockroaches that scuttle along its banks; the wisps of smoke that seem to rise from all directions. It's hard to believe that godforsaken spots like this can be found only a few miles from Sanctis's civilized paradise of Cabildo and Monroe.

Although at first the solitude appears total, it's possible to make out occasional shapes, too big to be dogs, outlined against the moonlit sky on top of the heaps—ragpickers at their work at this weird hour.

The jitters again, or something like the jitters, due this time not to the army or police but to this ghostly solitude, to this desolate, sinister world into which Sanctis is about to step.

He has the impression of a sort of small lake or lagoon among the hillocks, and he can just make out on what would be its right bank the tiny light of a possible cooking fire. Ragpickers brewing maté, he imagines, and he's trying to picture them taking a break around the fire, when there's a tap at his elbow and someone's telling him in a foreign accent, "Lacarra—next one, mister."

He wants to be polite and thank the man, but Sanctis is so surprised that his voice lets him down, coming out only in the form of a grunt or an idiot's stutter. Struggling to get up, he clumsily makes for the door on his swollen feet. The bus announces its imminent stop with the customary succession of fits and starts, until at last it rolls to a feeble halt with a growl that Sanctis finds more pitiful than ever.

Time to get out, but it wouldn't seem at all outlandish

to him to say goodbye to each of his companions first—with a warm handshake maybe, or a long, fond embrace. In the end he extends a farewell only to the one with the fair hair and sunken cheeks. Sanctis gives him a wave of the hand, which, although he means it sincerely, is a touch sentimental and affected—more appropriate for leaving an ocean liner or an airplane than a dilapidated local bus.

Setting one tentative foot on the pavement, then the other, Sanctis slowly lets himself off. It's as though he were cutting loose from Apollo IV or his own umbilical cord. For several seconds he stands there without moving an inch from the spot where his feet landed. A lump in his throat, he watches the bus move off in the direction of Puente Uriburu, its taillights growing smaller and smaller, the racket of the motor and bodywork—which by now seem the most familiar and cozy sounds in the world—growing fainter and fainter.

When the lights and the noise have faded for good, Sanctis looks around apprehensively, and the bewildering loneliness and helplessness which have beset him all along now overwhelm him as never before. He feels alone, he knows he's alone, about to do something the real meaning of which is not quite clear to him. But he's obeying a kind of call—he senses this—and bringing to a head that not quite intelligible scribble imprinted from the beginning, it seems, on the little page of his fate that pertains to Saturday the twelfth of November 1977, and of which Elena Vaccaro's telephone call in the late afternoon on Friday was a mere foretaste.

He realizes he's becoming caught up in wayward abstractions at just the worst moment, and his healthy reaction is to try to get back in touch with reality. Although the air still smells of burning garbage, the vast dumping grounds are now out of sight. What he sees instead is an unexpected mailbox and a widish street joining 27 de Febrero on the left and heading in toward Villa Soldati.

At the corner, on the front of a house overgrown with ivy, he makes out a sign reading "Lacarra." The street is by and large as he'd imagined it—houses of one story with corrugated iron roofs, privet hedges, and chinaberry trees. Sanctis looks for the first house number. He's in the 3700 block, on the even side of the street, and keeping to that side, he sets out toward number 4200.

For the hundredth time he wonders what the hell he'll do when he gets to 4225, and for the hundredth time he answers that he still has no idea. He keeps his eyes straight ahead in the direction of the five ill-lit blocks still between him and number 4225. There isn't a soul about, and the feel of the street is not at all reassuring. Maybe this is what decides him he must get this whole unpleasant business over with as soon as possible. He hurries his step, thinking sensibly and logically that since he's making his way to the house of a man to warn him that he's about to be abducted and must make an immediate getaway, it's crucial (if Sanctis actually means to do anything) that he act at once. Again he puts more spring in his step.

At the next corner, just as he's about to cross, a large gaunt mongrel, black in color and with the look of a killer, takes up a position in the middle of the road, baring its teeth, and growling in a low and thoroughly nasty way. That's all I need, a nice chunk out of my leg, Sanctis says to himself, feeling for a box of matches with which to ward the animal off. But before he can light and throw a single fiery stick, the dog, for reasons of its own, draws back, apparently seized by a sudden fright. Some ten yards off, it tries to recover its dignity, barking an outraged, harmless bark, to the accompaniment of which Sanctis manages to cross without trouble.

Sighing with relief as he quickens his pace again, he's now in the second block. But an automatic glance at the house fronts tells him he's in the 3600 block, which means that the numbers are running the other way. The 4200 block—damn it—has to be on the other side of the Riachuelo.

He quickly turns on his heel and is soon passing the black dog's corner again. The animal is now barking from afar to keep up a show, and Sanctis gets back to 27 de Febrero, wondering impatiently how he's going to cross the filthy concrete ditch of the Riachuelo without an enormous detour.

As he scouts around uncertainly in search of a would-be bridge, he looks over at the extension of Lacarra Street on the other bank. The left-hand sidewalk there looks more or less the same as here—low houses, hedges, chinaberry trees, etc. But on the right side, he sees the start of a very high wall that's illuminated at regular intervals. At the risk of slipping and falling into the stinking black water, Sanctis gets as close to the

edge as he can and peers across. It's a military installa-
tion of some sort. In black letters up on the side of a
yellow water tank he can just catch the word ARSENAL.

This is getting more and more complicated, he thinks.
Trying to pass by there at this hour is strictly out of the
question. Sentries nowadays don't beat around the bush,
and to be pumped full of lead free of charge is hardly in
his best interests. Sanctis will have to give the place a
wide berth, but first he has to cross the Riachuelo. Yes,
but where? There isn't a bridge in sight, and along this
whole stretch of the river you wouldn't expect to find a
boat.

His only option is to carry on to Puente Uriburu—on
foot, naturally, as there's no hope of a bus around here at
this hour. He takes a couple of deep breaths to work
himself up to it, adjusts his belt, and sets off.

He walks alongside the Riachuelo, on the narrow concrete strip that borders the water, his feet crunching a
thin layer of dried mud. It takes a mental effort not to let
himself be caught up by the sensation of unreality or
nightmare produced in him by this unearthly place and
by finding himself here alone, on the edge of a vast concrete ditch, trudging—perhaps to his perdition—among
endless heaps of garbage, distant guttering fires, strange
gurgling sounds, and on every hand wisps of smoke that
betray no visible source.

In an effort to stave off this unreality, Sanctis stops,
picks up a couple of clods, and flings them into the canal. Like a boy, he stands there watching the two series
of concentric circles spread out over the dark surface.

Growing larger and larger, they merge, and now, almost invisible, they still show themselves, gentle ripples lapping the shore.

But the action does not have the salutary effect Sanctis had hoped for. For some reason, his eye begins seeing corpses dumped into the murky waters from the opposite bank and then sinking and sending out these same concentric circles—but grown to monstrous proportions.

He walks on, reckoning that if he keeps up a good pace he can get to Puente Uriburu in fifteen minutes. He lengthens his stride and makes for a string of lights he takes to be Sáenz Avenue.

He is three hundred yards along when he hears behind him the creak of wheels and the slow trot of a horse. A cart looms out of the dark into the light of a street lamp, a man standing astride the driving box. Although Sanctis is fairly certain that Charon went about in a boat and not in what appears to be a fruit vendor's rickety old cart, this strange, almost dreamlike apparition sends a shudder through him. Sanctis stops and gapes.

As the cart passes, the driver, a young man in a cap, an incredible waistcoat, and a black sash around his middle, gives a friendly wave of the hand and wishes Sanctis a good night. Sanctis notes that the boy speaks with an accent from one of the northern provinces. Heartened by the friendliness (he must have taken Sanctis for a lone ragpicker), Sanctis returns the greeting as a roundabout approach to asking for a lift. Stepping forward and keep-

ing his voice casual, he wants to know about the nearest
bridge over the canal.

The young man reins in his decrepit horse and says
straight out, "Where are you going, brother?"

The word "brother" spoken in these circumstances
both moves Sanctis and fills him with gratitude, and he
has to steady his voice before half stammering, "Uh . . .
to Lacarra Street. I mean, the extension of Lacarra." And
he points in the direction of the arsenal wall.

"Lacarra Street," the boy wonders aloud, realizing
from Sanctis's appearance that he's not a member of the
guild.

"Yes, sure, 4200 Lacarra. It must be there on the other
side of the Riachuelo."

"No, that can't be," says the boy, his tone still
friendly. "Lacarra Street ends right here."

"What do you mean, it ends right here?" says Sanctis,
his heart beginning to thump.

"Well, yes, it ends here at the Riachuelo. It doesn't
continue on the other side," the boy says with assurance.

"What about that street over there, then? Where the
arsenal is." Sanctis is trying to confirm a suspicion, and
he desperately wants to hear one particular answer.

"That's not Lacarra. It's José María Moreno," answers
the boy, untroubled by what might seem disbelief on the
part of this apparently confused guy. Clicking his
tongue, the young man gets his nag moving again.

"Oh, is that right?" Sanctis exclaims as if he'd just

heard the revelation of the century. A smile lighting up his face, he adds a hearty "Thanks!" that could just as easily have been "Thank God!"

Because now everything seems patently clear. For the good of Sanctis's inner peace and the safety of his neck, it turns out that the address the intelligence agencies have for Bernardo Lipstein—and that mysteriously came to Elena Vaccaro's ears—is even more false than Judas's soul. Obviously, Bernardo Lipstein was smart enough to pass this address on to someone someplace at some time, foreseeing just such an eventuality as this one tonight.

In other words, when the fucking Ford Falcons descend on number 4225 Lacarra Street, they're going to have to piss around this garbage dump a good long while, the same way Sanctis did. And then, Jesus, are they going to be in for the letdown of their lives!

The cart's moved off; Sanctis, having forgotten to ask for a lift to Puente Uriburu, waves a hand. A sweet joy floods his heart, and suddenly he feels well, fantastically well, and not a bit tired. Because it's all over now, and, jitters or no, for God or his conscience or just for the hell of it, he's done what he had to do. And because in the end everything turned out to be so easy. And because more than likely Julio Cardini's address on Álvarez Thomas is as unlocatable and fallacious as this one was.

CHAPTER XVI

In which, despite the poignant love songs that accompany Sanctis all the way from Nueva Pompeya to Villa Urquiza like some wandering music of the spheres, a number of unaccountable things are still going on

And now Francisco Sanctis's story, which began at five o'clock in the afternoon on the eleventh of November 1977 with a phone call from out of the blue indeed seems to be drawing to a close.

We have only to see Sanctis sprawled on the back seat of a taxi, breathing nervously, smoking his thirty-eighth king-size Imparcial of the night, and looking up at the beautiful sky over Triunvirato where it crosses Avenida de los Incas, to sense that the inevitable end is nearly at hand.

After his heartfelt exchange with the young carter from Tucumán, after his metaphysical struggle with God and his conscience, and a feeling that came from his balls, Sanctis set out with a bouncier step to cover the fifteen or twenty blocks to Puente Uriburu. Once there, he hied off down Sáenz Avenue, his eye peeled for a highly improbable taxi.

At this point, the sly joker, who has been and evidently still is directing Sanctis's footsteps, comes to the rescue and conjures up a real taxi (complete with four wheels, a driver, a motor, a Saint Christopher medallion, and a few cassettes of the Brazilian pop star Roberto Carlos). This vehicle nosed its way out of Colmo Street, entering Sáenz Avenue both magically and strictly against the flow of traffic, just as Sanctis's antennae were anxiously sweeping the avenue a block away at Echauri Street. And the aforementioned sly joker, of whom we've heard so much in this story, arranged it that the cabbie, a fattish man with steel-rimmed spectacles, gray hair, and the air of a patriarch or Santa Claus, would clearly hear (in spite of the million friends Roberto Carlos is calling out for) the frantic SOS of Sanctis whistling him up, two fingers in his mouth, from the corner of Echauri. The driver would then pull his car to the curb in a nice civilized fashion so that this guy trotting down Sáenz Avenue, puffing and panting and paddling his hands like a drowning man, could get in.

The foregoing facts are as mysterious and hard to believe as the unexpected appearance of the 28 bus at Puente Saavedra, or the sudden backing off of a fearsome, murderous hound who owned a stretch of sidewalk along Lacarra Street, but they are all strictly true, and consequently Sanctis finds himself riding in a taxi, listening to a third Roberto Carlos cassette, furtively patting his wallet in fear that he's not going to have the

174

money to pay for this long ride from one end of the city to the other, and about to arrive, as far as we know, at number 2837 Álvarez Thomas Avenue. That is, at the second address memorized in the Renault—that is, the home of one Julio Cardini, the second of those condemned to death by Air Force Intelligence, or perhaps only by the feverish imagination of Elenita Vaccaro, who, as we all know, has an affinity for melodramas of this sort. But for the time being none of these uncertainties can be cleared up.

Nor, at this stage of the game, does Sanctis really care much about these uncertainties. Meaning that the address on Álvarez Thomas, toward which he's now heading, lulled by sweet Brazilian tones, may exist or may be as fictitious as the elusive, super-clever Bernardo Lipstein's. Julio Cardini himself may exist in the flesh, or he may be only the figment of a crazy woman's imagination. What does exist, on the other hand—here and now and more alive than the acacia trees along Triunvirato Avenue or the back of Santa Claus's plump neck or the honeyed gush of Roberto Carlos or that vague anxiety that has been an inseparable part of Francisco Sanctis for some time now—is this inexplicable need, this blind impulse to bring to a conclusion what started that night with Elena Vaccaro's proposal but may also have to do with something else. What else? Well, with some sort of ancient command or of an immutable moment that Sanctis has perhaps intuited or foreseen or wished for all his life. The moment lying in wait for him—beyond his account books or his desk with the view of Avenida de

Mayo or María Angélica's cozy warmth or the children's homework or his journeys on the 60 bus—and toward which in some strange way he knew he was aiming. This moment is a figurative tick mark in the book of fate, a door he must pass through, a threshold, a cross-roads—something no one is making any claim to explain rationally.

And least of all, of course, poor Francisco Sanctis. But it would be wrong not to admit that in his own way (which just now he couldn't have communicated for all the world) Sanctis senses that this command, tick mark, throwing down of the gauntlet, or whatever, is intimately linked with the best and most enduring part of himself. With something he once connected with God. With something intuited during his adolescence and come upon again for an instant at work while thinking about something else or while listening at home to the second movement of a certain quartet on a lonely rainy Sunday.

He knows perfectly well that it's not hard to sidestep the little door, to ignore the challenge, and that as a result the world won't come to an end. But he also knows that should he not pass through that door, should he not grapple with this moment, his moment, all the other moments of his life would unaccountably and suddenly lose their meaning. There is a Francisco Sanctis—no one denies this—pitifully gnawed by doubts and fears; but at the same time there is another Francisco Sanctis, dedicated and courageous, who knows what he's doing, who on certain occasions lends support to his other, indecisive, tired, and scared self.

Scared, naturally, because although it's true that some of his uncertainties have miraculously vanished into thin air, what hasn't vanished but still clings to him like a leech is his old sidekick, anxiety. The clammy draft that nestled between his skin and his shirt from the moment he first heard Elena Vaccaro's batty story there in the semidarkness of the Renault is still with him and shows no sign of going away.

This attack of the jitters, however, is slightly different from previous ones. Why? Because now when something, some sprite, some tiny voice, is whispering in his ear and telling him that at this stage it won't be easy to back out, now when it's fairly certain that with or without rubbery legs or icy knot in the stomach or this uncontrollable urge to pee that's suddenly come over him, he will make his way to Julio Cardini's door and tell him what he has to tell him—now, oddly, his jitters are accompanied by an unexpected feeling of power and fulfillment, maybe even of an inexplicable and impromptu joy.

None of which stops his voice from going all shaky and throaty when, just as Roberto Carlos is thanking the Lord for a load of hogwash, Sanctis notices that the taxi's driving along Álvarez Thomas somewhere in the 2000 block. This sends him leaning forward to tell his bulky driver to stop right there at the corner of Echeverría. This sudden countercommand provokes in Santa

Claus neither a response nor an expression of surprise, in spite of the fact that when his voluble passenger got into the taxi he clearly stated, "Álvarez Thomas 2800."

Quite the contrary. Santa Claus brakes smoothly just a yard past Echeverría, ceremoniously lifts his steel-rimmed glasses, sticks his face up to the meter, and in a voice somewhere between a fruit peddler and Carlos Gardel he cheerily sings out the fare before embarking upon a long, contagious yawn.

Sanctis, who a while ago was afraid he wasn't going to have enough money (in which case his only recourse would have been to try coming to a rather tricky agreement with the fat man), smack in the middle of the yawn contracted from Santa Claus makes a quick but thorough tally of the contents of his wallet, including every last coin in his pockets. And what comes of it? Once again, something as incredible and uncanny as the incredible, uncanny appearance of a certain heaven-sent bus at two o'clock in the morning or the mysterious backing off of a wild beast that seemed on the point of making a meal of him—namely this: the loot, all that he's rustled up out of his innermost pockets, is just enough to cover the fare, including a barely acceptable tip. In other words, having got out of the taxi, said good night to the cabbie, and shut the door, Sanctis finds himself stone broke.

But the funniest part is that the irritating fact of being miles from home without a dime to his name on this occasion causes Sanctis not the slightest tickle of unease or anger. As a matter of fact, it might be said that right now going around penniless gives him a wonderful feeling of lightness and freedom, one could almost say of nakedness or—pardon the expression—purity. As if, by an act fluctuating somewhere between superstition and religion, he considered it necessary, or at least auspicious, to divest himself of all his worldly wealth before facing the ordeal ahead.

So that, pockets and maybe soul, too, rid of all impedimenta (and having taken a piss against a small dark wall along Echeverría Street), Sanctis makes straight for the 2800 block of Álvarez Thomas.

Thank goodness the avenue is well lighted. There are no foul smoke screens or impenetrable shadows or fearful black dogs to attack the passerby.

He breathes deeply. He feels fine. It could be the first time he's really felt fine since he left Elena Vaccaro there at the curb on Olleros Street and set out upon his road to Calvary.

The vague fear that subtly wraps him in a web injects into his bloodstream the exact dose of adrenaline to keep him, despite tiredness, awake and on his toes.

Now and again (still), he feels the impulse to quit, to head nonchalantly down the next side street, or without further ado just to turn on his heel. Nonetheless, his step relatively firm considering the number of miles he's covered tonight, he marches on down the lighted sidewalk of Álvarez Thomas.

What can he be thinking about? The probable idiotic act he's about to commit? His past? María Angélica? God? His desk at Luchini & Monsreal's? Julio Cardini's expression, which Sanctis may never get to see? Julio Cardini's life, which idiotically depends on Sanctis's mud-caked shoes and whether or not they keep striding, deliberately and rhythmically, in the same line that they have been striding? The shower he'll take when he gets home? His sweaty feet? Death? No one can say.

It's really hard to tell exactly what's in his head at this moment. More than hard. Perhaps the writer, who set out to tell Francisco Sanctis's story and who thereby also risks committing an idiotic act, doesn't really want to know himself. For whatever reason.

It's true that the more or less psychological nature, etc., of this book was mentioned at the outset. But for God's sake, there's a limit to things. And in this case the limit probably concerns a certain respect or certain decorum or even just a wise old law of the streets that proscribes idle speculation about a guy whose one and only interest lies in the course he's pursuing. Would anyone have had the dimwitted idea of trying to find out what on earth Sergeant Cabral was thinking when, back during the South American wars of independence, he risked his neck plucking General San Martín out from under his fallen horse? Would the fact that the good sergeant from Corrientes had been thinking about his wife or his country or a whore he met the night before in a San Lorenzo brothel or the injured foot of the young general with the Spanish accent (who would have been butchered like a young bull had someone not acted promptly) or a gambling debt or anything else have in any way changed the significance or consequence of his valiant deed? That's the thing.

For once, let us not meddle in Sanctis's privacy. Let us not pry into what is none of our business, and instead watch Sanctis, apparently calm, his fear conquered, preceded by his shifting shadow, walking alone down the broad sidewalk of Álvarez Thomas Avenue.

He slows down a bit now, swings his arms, thrusts his head forward, from time to time rubs his right cheek as if it were itching. And that's all. Let us not add a word to these simple facts. He's doing what he must do. Simply doing what he must do. His step calm, almost reluctant, he's going to an old rendezvous with destiny.

Therefore it's not Sanctis's place to speak. What has he to say? What can he say? Really, it's for someone else to speak for him now. To speak? Yes, why not? Let us keep back a respectful distance and assume the trivial though rather risky role that's ours in this affair. That is, setting aside all our typically Buenos Aires circumspection, call a spade a spade, and without either reserve or shame dare state a fact as simple as that something is taking place here in these placid middle-class streets in Villa Urquiza, among old acacias, rubbish bins, pretty little houses, and the silent padding of some cat on the prowl—something serious, something we don't want to explain too closely, because all explanation turns out either obvious or didactic or plain foolish. Instead, at this point we would like our little conversational aside to take on a deeper, more responsive, more epic note in

181

order to be able to say there goes Francisco Sanctis and to look at him, know him, understand his long, confused night, and see a triumph of his humanity in all this—in his tiredness, in his undeniable fear, in his sweaty arm-pits and feet, and in his obstinate determination to stick to his course, to go on being a man, a humble Christ and a Christian, a man on foot, a man simply going to his old rendezvous, finding himself perhaps for all time, being born anew, knowing at last that he is Francisco Sanctis, finding out his true name. All in this absurd lonely walk through a sleeping city that isn't even aware of his presence.

Yes, yes, very interesting, but the fact is that there's not much time left for this sort of digression. Life goes on, and Sanctis, who has continued walking while we've been bumbling on, has just arrived at number 2837.

He stops now outside a modest six- or seven-story building, lifts his eyes, and sees the number on a ceramic plaque set slightly askew in the wall. In the entrance he also notices a small lobby or alcove with plastic ferns and geraniums in a long planter, the door buzzers in rows along one side, and a big glass door through which a dark interior can be seen. Against the side of the building is the partly dilapidated, partly rebuilt wall of a construction site.

Sanctis backs away from the entrance a few steps and for no particular reason stares up at the third floor. There's a window with the blinds down, and not a single light is burning on any floor of the building. No matter, because apartment C has to be around the back, so looking things over from here doesn't make a lot of sense.

Again he approaches the building. Again he casts a glance along both sides of the street. His hands feel clammy.

Entering the lobby, he stands in front of the intercom system, hangs back for a second or two, and, perhaps not altogether aware of what he's doing, he suddenly places an index finger on the button belonging to apartment 3-C.

He waits. Automatically, he rummages around in his pocket, and in relief he turns up his last Imparcial, half squashed down at the bottom of the pack. Bringing the cigarette to his lips, he makes a screen with both hands, and lights it. He sucks in long and pleasurably. In the glass door, the reflected glow of the cigarette becomes more intense. Sanctis picks a shred of tobacco off his tongue, blows out the smoke, and tilts his head to one side.

Because of this old habit of tilting his head, because of the way he slumps his shoulders in relaxation, it's obvious that he still hasn't seen the two shadows emerging from behind the elevator nor the car slowly drawing up from Olazábal Street nor the glint of the gun barrel pointing at him from the darkness of the building site next door.

CHAPTER XVII

NAME	AGE	OCCU-PATION	ABDUCTED
Sánchez Cáceres, Gladys	27	employee	San Juan, 1 Mar 1977
Sánchez de Repetti, Elina	23	teaching assistant	Buenos Aires, 31 Jul 1976
Sánchez, Fernando	34	employee	Buenos Aires, 23 Sept 1977
Sánchez, Hugo Ramón	25	employee	Córdoba, 24 Apr 1977
Sánchez, María Matilde	27	psychologist	Buenos Aires, 10 Jul 1976
Sánchez, Modesto Bibiano	40	public employee	Tucumán, 29 Mar 1976
.Sanctis, Francisco Nicodemo	41	bookkeeper	Buenos Aires, 12 Nov 1977
Sandoval, Juan Carlos	36	manual worker	Buenos Aires, 1 Jul 1977
Sandoval, Pedro	33	laborer	Buenos Aires, 1 Jul 1977
Sangiorgio, Carlos Andrés	26	lawyer	Buenos Aires, 24 Aug 1977
Sanglas, Ricardo Antonio	19	student	La Plata, 15 Jun 1977
Sanmartín, Daniel	22	laborer	Río Ceballos, 29 Mar 1976
Santoro, Roberto Jorge	38	teacher-poet	Buenos Aires, 1 Jun 1977

Source: Amnesty International